BOOST

BOOST

BY KATHY MACKEL

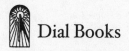 Dial Books

DIAL BOOKS
A member of Penguin Group (USA) Inc.
Published by The Penguin Group
Penguin Group (USA) Inc., 375 Hudson Street, New York, NY 10014, U.S.A.

Penguin Group (Canada), 90 Eglinton Avenue East, Suite 700, Toronto, Ontario, Canada M4P 2Y3 (a division of Pearson Penguin Canada Inc.) • Penguin Books Ltd, 80 Strand, London WC2R 0RL, England • Penguin Ireland, 25 St. Stephen's Green, Dublin 2, Ireland (a division of Penguin Books Ltd) • Penguin Group (Australia), 250 Camberwell Road, Camberwell, Victoria 3124, Australia (a division of Pearson Australia Group Pty Ltd) • Penguin Books India Pvt Ltd, 11 Community Centre, Panchsheel Park, New Delhi - 110 017, India • Penguin Group (NZ), 67 Apollo Drive, Rosedale, North Shore 0632, New Zealand (a division of Pearson New Zealand Ltd) • Penguin Books (South Africa) (Pty) Ltd, 24 Sturdee Avenue, Rosebank, Johannesburg 2196, South Africa • Penguin Books Ltd, Registered Offices: 80 Strand, London WC2R 0RL, England

Designed by Nancy R. Leo-Kelly
Text set in Hoefler text
Printed in the U.S.A.
5 7 9 10 8 6

Library of Congress Cataloging-in-Publication Data
Mackel, Kathryn, date.
Boost / by Kathy Mackel.
p. cm.
Summary: Thirteen-year-old Savvy's dreams of starting for her
elite basketball team are in danger when she is accused of taking steroids.
ISBN 978-0-8037-3240-7
[1. Basketball—Fiction. 2. Steroids—Fiction.] I. Title.
PZ7.M1955Bo 2008 [Fic]—dc22 2007049441

To Patrick "Murph" Murphy,
the best friend any girl athlete could have

O⇒O⇒O⇒O⇒

Acknowledgments

I owe a big thank-you to my Writer's Group—the two Daves, Bev, Patty, Bob, Lee, and Kathy—for cheering me on. I got a big boost from my editor, Liz Waniewski, whose wisdom and skill are a real *swish*. As always, I'm grateful to the two men who make my work possible, my agent, Lee Hough, and—last but always best—my husband, Steve.

BOOST

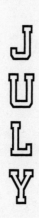

CHAPTER ONE

I stood at the free throw line, all eyes on me.

Chill, I told myself. Forget that these were tryouts for an elite 16U basketball team. Forget that I didn't know a soul here. Forget that I was the only girl on the floor and everyone else was watching.

I felt the ball, leather like second skin, and bent my knees, loose and strong. Powering up through my legs, I flexed my wrists and watched the ball take flight.

Swish.

A murmur went through the coaches, parents, and the other girls. They would be saying, *Who is that girl, where did she come from,* and *how the heck tall is she?*

Savvy Christopher. Newly arrived in Rhode Island, all the way from New Mexico. Six feet two and growing.

I had made seven baskets in a row in this shoot-around drill. Two from the baseline, four from the blocks, and one from the free throw line—all net. Now it was time to show my stuff from the three-point range.

Eighteen girls had shot before me, but only one—a dark-eyed girl who moved like a cat—had made the seven shots necessary to get to the perimeter. She took the basket straight on from the top of the key and bricked her shot.

Time to beat Dark Eyes.

I moved to the corner baseline. A perfect shot comes from

good mechanics and good practice, but it's focus that buys the basket. Just me, the ball, and that hoop.

I bounced the ball once and let it fly. More music, the sweet sigh of all net.

Someone on the bleachers clapped. Others joined in before Coach Murphy barked out, "No."

Even though each girl went out to the floor alone, we weren't there to put on a show. The point of this drill was to show how we performed under pressure.

I made four more baskets before I missed—a spinner that flirted with the rim before it toppled off. The air seemed to go out of the gym, as if everyone had been holding their breath. I grabbed my rebound, tossed it to the next girl, then sat down. No eye contact with the crowd, no smile, no ego. No attitude to show up the other girls.

Dark Eyes squeezed in next to me. "Yo, dude. Sweet shooting."

I shrugged. "Thanks. You too."

"You new here?"

"We moved last month from New Mexico."

"I'm Nina Gonzalez. Gonzo to my friends."

"I'm Savvy Christopher," I said, tapping her fist.

"How old are you?"

"I'll be fourteen in August. Going into eighth grade. You?"

"Thirteen until Columbus Day. Ditto on the eighth grade."

"You don't want to play fourteen-under?" I said. "The cut-off is Labor Day, so you'd be eligible."

"No way. In fact . . ." Gonzo gave me a sly smile. "I have a better idea. Wanna hear?"

We grabbed our bags and crossed the street to the high school, Gonzo chattering like a chipmunk. "Check it out, dude. We need to become instant best friends, because when we walk into those tryouts, those older girls will try to chew us up."

"Yeah, sure." My head spun. My parents had dropped me off at the 16U tryouts—I never let them stay—and suddenly, I had a new best friend and an itch to make the 18s.

"I got three sisters, one brother, all older than me," Gonzo said. "My mother is a nurse, so I can't ever fake a sick day. My father is a commercial fisherman and we have stupid cod three times a week and I stupid hate it. I love pizza and lime soda—"

"Oh puke."

"Not at the same time, dude. What else? Oh yeah, I got this thing for blond guys with big shoulders. Chick flicks where someone dies turn my stomach. And, in case you couldn't guess, I love basketball more than anything."

"Yeah, I got that," I said, laughing.

"You?"

"I have one sister, who is almost sixteen."

"She play ball?"

"No, she used to be a gymnast but now she's a cheerleader."

"She tall like you?"

"She's a shrimp. About your size," I said. "No offense."

"No problem. People don't see me coming."

"Cool. We moved here in early June so Callie could try out for the high school squad. My father used to golf on the PGA tour—"

"Whoa!"

My stomach churned. Back home everyone knew, so I'd never had to say this aloud before. "That's in the past. Injuries and all that. He's in college now, studying business. My mother sells printing supplies. We live with my father's aunt on her sheep farm. Okay, what else? I love action movies but freakin' hate those torture movies."

"Guys?"

I laughed. "They all gotta grow up first."

As we crossed an outdoor court, Gonzo jumped and ruffled the net. Not to be outdone, I leaped and touched the rim. Someday—maybe soon—I would dunk one.

"And I love basketball more than anything," I said.

"All right!" Gonzo spun into some handshake more complicated than a hip-hop routine. Okay, I thought. If nothing else, I won't be bored anymore.

We went inside and got in line to register.

"Can I have your forms please?" The lady behind the table wore red reading glasses that matched her flaming red hair. Hopefully, it was a dye job. Surely Mother Nature couldn't be that cruel.

"We left our forms at the middle school gym, at the sixteens tryouts," I said. "We didn't know we'd need to bring them with us."

"I'm sorry, but the organization doesn't allow girls to try out for more than one team."

"We're not trying out for the sixteens anymore," Gonzo said. "We decided to try out for this team."

A tall girl with broad shoulders glanced up from lacing her

high-tops. Sheesh, I thought. Someone still wears high-tops to play basketball?

"What grade are you two in, anyway?" Shoulders said.

"Eighth," I mumbled.

"This team is for high school players."

Gonzo wagged her finger at the girl. "No, dude. It's for girls eighteen years old and under."

Shoulders made a *pfffftt*-ing sound and went into the gym.

"Perhaps you don't understand," Red Glasses said. "This is an elite team. We've got excellent players from all over the county trying to make it. There's even a couple of girls from eastern Connecticut. Your best bet is to go back to the six-teens, where you'll be comfortable."

My knees wobbled. I was in no mood for a reality check two thousand miles from home.

Gonzo dug her elbow into my side. We'd been friends for ten minutes and she already could read my mind. "We want challenge, not comfort," she said. "That's why we're here, ma'am."

Red Glasses looked up at me, then adjusted her gaze a foot lower to Gonzo. "Fine. Go over to the middle school and pull your registration from the Flames. But understand this—once you commit to trying out for Fire, there's no going back. If you don't make this team, you won't be on any team. I'd advise you to think this through very carefully."

As we jogged back across the street, Gonzo said, "You thinking it through ve-r-r-ry carefully?"

"You heard the lady. We go for the eighteens and don't make it, we're screwed."

Gonzo stopped in the middle of the road. A car beeped as it whizzed by, but she didn't even blink. "I took you for a gamer, Savvy."

"I am a gamer."

"Then stop chewing your hair and let's do this."

At the middle school, the guy at the check-in table gave us a big smile. "You're back! We didn't know where you had gone."

I hadn't expected to be greeted like a superstar prospect. I stood there, a six-foot-two lump of stupid.

"Could we have our registration forms, please?" Gonzo said. "Gonzalez and Christopher."

The man gave us the same once-over Red Glasses had but without the sneer. "Why do you girls want your forms?"

"Because we're trying out for the eighteens."

His eyes went wide. "Oh, please don't. The sixteens need you."

Clearly the 18U Fire wouldn't need me. But suddenly, I needed them because I needed to be the best I could be. The 18s were the team to make that happen.

"Sorry," I said. "Good luck with your season."

CHAPTER TWO

We handed in our registrations, pinned numbers to our shirts, and marched into tryouts for the 18U Kent County Fire.

Gonzo walked right up to the girl with the broad shoulders. "Hey, dude. This is Savvy. And I'm Gonzo."

"Not to be rude," Shoulders said, "but since you shouldn't be here, I'm going to pretend you're not."

"Ouch," I said.

"Fine. We're not here to make friends anyway. Right, Savvy? We've got plenty of those."

Maybe she did, but all my friends were back in New Mexico. There was no one to hang with at Aunt Betty's farm except for my sister, Callie. The first week we were here, she spent every minute on her cell phone, talking with her friends back home. Then she stopped calling them, saying she'd never see them again anyway. These days all she wanted to do was veg out on her top bunk, eat junk food, and listen to her iPod.

Making the 16s would have been a slam dunk, giving me eleven instant friends. Would Gonzo still be my pal if we both bombed? The bigger question was—if I didn't make the team, could I live without playing basketball until the school season began in December? I needed basketball as much as I needed eating and sleeping.

But why settle for a dried-up hamburger on a stale bun when you've got a shot at a juicy steak?

The coach introduced himself to the group. An older guy with a stumpy build, Mr. Fitzgerald looked more like a baseball catcher than a basketball geek. He started us with the standard drills and, for the first time since leaving the other tryouts, the worry worm in my belly took a knee.

Even though the suicide splits were our second set of the day, Gonzo beat everyone and I finished pretty high in the pack. I aced the layups from the right side and faked my way through the left.

In the dribbling drills, Gonzo slipped ghostlike through any wall the defense could put up. I was more like a fly in a spider's web, getting tangled with each move I tried to make. My feet were growing so fast, they didn't know right from left most of the time.

I dominated in the three-on-three defensive drills, my octopus arms claiming all the real estate under the basket. At one point, Shoulders deked at me, and then faded back for a jumper. I leaped, blocked, and smashed the ball. Right into her face.

Oops—no way to make friends.

Gonzo buried her face in her shirt, she was laughing so hard as I tried to apologize.

"This is tryouts," Shoulders mumbled through an ice pack. "Not the NBA finals. Lighten up."

"Like I'd do that," I muttered to Gonzo. "I play hard all the time, even in my home court."

"You have a home court?"

When we lived in New Mexico, we had a full-sized court

with expensive Plexiglas boards, a drinking fountain, and a cabana with a bathroom. The swimming pool and hot tub were next to the court.

Now it all belonged to the bank.

Mr. Fitzgerald whistled us back to the three-on-threes, saving me from having to answer. Now that I was on offense, the hoop seemed as big as a backyard swimming pool. After sinking my fourth three-pointer, a girl with a long black ponytail yelled at me, "This isn't all about you, rookie. Pass the stupid ball already."

I didn't bother to point out that neither she nor the skinny blond girl on my "three" had bothered to pass to me.

After the break, we scrimmaged. As long as Gonzo fed me balls, I sunk shot after shot. As soon as I had to dribble in traffic, I was such a gawk that I might as well have been wearing clown shoes and a snowsuit. I fouled out with six minutes left in the scrimmage.

"That girl is a train wreck," Shoulders said to Ponytail.

I slumped on the bench and worried she was right.

○≡○≡○≡○≡

"I'll watch the video, check my notes, then make my decision," Mr. Fitzgerald said. "You'll all get a call tonight."

Gonzo tapped my fist. "My mom's here, so I gotta run. You got my number, right?"

"Yeah." We had entered them into each other's cell phones.

"Call me, okay? After the coach calls and congratulates you."

Right. Anyone could see that Gonzo had made the team and I had made the stupidest mistake of my life. I grabbed my bag and headed for the door.

"Christopher. Hold up." Mr. Fitzgerald waved me to the middle of the gym. Best place for privacy because no one could listen from behind a bleacher or around a corner. Best place to tell me how I had bombed this afternoon.

He popped a piece of gum into his mouth. "Want one?"

"No thanks, Mr. Fitzgerald."

"The gals just call me Fitz. Not Fitzie, not Mister. Just Fitz." As bald as a soccer ball, he had watery blue eyes that almost disappeared under dust-bunny eyebrows. "I gotta say this, Christopher—you are the most talented girl I've ever seen at a tryout."

"I am?"

His *pfftt* was music to my ear. "Yeah. A player like you doesn't come along often. Maybe not ever in most coaches' careers."

I could barely breathe. "Wow. Thanks."

"Don't thank me yet. Gal, are you ever raw. Whoever coached you out west must have thought they were coaching football, because you stagger around the court like a fullback."

The guy had launched me into the rafters, only to yank me down and grind me underfoot.

"Your height is a huge asset but you're skinny," Fitz said. "Easy to push around. You've got the best shot I've seen in some time. Heck, you shoot the lights out. But you're a gunner."

Call me ugly, call me stupid, but don't call me a gunner. "I'm sorry. I'm kind of used to having to carry a team."

"That's not what this game—or this team—is about."

I bit my lower lip to keep it from trembling. "I know."

"What do you want out of playing with us, Christopher?"

"I want the chance to play the game right."

"Hm."

"And . . ." I searched for the right flavor of crap he would swallow. "To be the best, you've got to play with the best."

"Hm."

"Okay. Screw that," I said, my ears hot. "I want to play hard and win hard. I want to push it all the time. That's what I want."

Fitz smiled. "We don't call this team Fire for nothing, gal."

He glanced at Red Glasses, who pretended to be arranging her paperwork, then back to me, staring up because I topped him by a good four or five inches. "I'll catch some flak for putting the Gonzalez girl on the team, but we have a big hole for point guard, one she'll fill. But if I put you on, I'll catch hell. You understand that?"

"I guess."

"Let me hear why, then."

"You take me, you cut someone who expected to make the team. Someone . . ." I took a deep breath. ". . . someone older than me and maybe better prepared to play at this level."

"Good. What else?"

I dug my nails into my palms. Why didn't he just tell me he didn't want me? "Maybe you'd have to cut someone who played for you last year. Someone you know well, whose parents you know."

"You see the tough position I'm in. But let's say I take you on this team. Now *you're* in a tough position."

"I am?"

"You're starting potential but you're not starting material, no way. Your playing time will be limited unless you can boost your game."

"I'm a hard worker," I said.

"Sometimes it takes more than hard work."

"Like what?"

He rubbed his face. "Listen, Christopher—I called over to Pat Murphy. He wants you on the sixteens so desperately that he browbeat the board of directors. They agreed to pretend that you didn't leave his tryout to come to mine. That's what you should do. Play for Murph, get some solid coaching, and come back next year."

"Do I get a choice?" I said.

"You mean, will I put you on this team if you want to go for it?"

"Yeah."

Fitz snorted. "I don't see how I could keep you off."

"Then, Coach . . ." I said with a smile, "I'll look forward to your call tonight."

CHAPTER THREE

Fitz called me around seven o'clock. "Last chance to go back to the sixteens, Christopher."

"No, thank you," I said.

"Prepare to work your butt off then."

I danced downstairs and told my family.

"Last year you played fourteen and under," Mom said. "Are you sure you want to jump two age brackets?"

"Of course she's sure," my father said. "This is terrific."

Aunt Betty looked up from her livestock magazine and gave me a crinkly smile. "I'm pleased for you, Savannah."

Later that evening, my sister, Callie, presented me with a cake that she had baked in a bowl so it was shaped like a basketball. She decorated it with caramel frosting and used chocolate sprinkles for the laces. She liked her handiwork so much, she ate two pieces.

Gonzo called, so jazzed that we talked until after midnight. I went to sleep with a dumb grin on my face but a knot in my belly. My family thought I was a superstar but my coach—and me too, I guess—knew I had a lot to prove.

In the middle of the night, coyotes howled so loud that both Callie and I woke up.

My sister pressed her hands against her ears. "Do those things have to be so loud?"

Deep in the woods, *those things* screeched like someone was twisting their heads off. Hot on the scent of some poor critter, they'd soon be the ones doing the twisting. The clock read 3:55 A.M., a time when all respectable creatures should be calling it a night.

I had my first practice tomorrow. I needed to be sharp. But between the coyotes howling and my sister complaining, I couldn't get back to sleep.

Coyotes only rate halfway up my sister's list of fearsome things. Spiders, brown toads, and slimy slugs totally creep her out. Snakes terrify her so much that she screams at coiled garden hoses and brightly colored ropes.

There's only one thing I'm afraid of: I refuse to even think about not playing basketball—that might jinx it into happening.

"Savvy, they're getting closer," Callie said.

We parted the curtains in time to see shadows streak across the yard. The coyotes cut across the driveway, heading for the sheep.

"Shouldn't we do something?"

"No, Sultana will chase them off," I said. Any moment we'd hear the German shepherd's warning bark and those flea-bitten fiends would run back into the brush like the cowards they were.

We listened for a full minute, imagining the worst. All we heard was silence. Finally Callie said, "Good," and climbed back up on the top bunk.

When we heard the gunshot half a minute later, we knew it wasn't good. Not good at all.

We found Aunt Betty on her back in the dew-soaked pasture.

"Blasted fleabags. I'll drill holes in every last one of them." As she tried to stand, her eyes fluttered so only the whites showed. She collapsed against my father with an *oomph*.

"Daddy, are you okay?" Callie said. With three fused disks in his back and two in his neck, our father wasn't supposed to lift anything heavier than a loaf of bread.

"I'm fine, Cal. Really." He rubbed his jacket in the wet grass and pressed it against Aunt Betty's forehead. She moaned but didn't come out of her faint.

I shuffled him out of the way so I could raise Aunt Betty into a sitting position. Though she was almost as tall as me, she felt like a china plate you could break simply by clinking a fork against it.

"Ohmigosh," I said, pointing. "How did she do *that*?"

Aunt Betty's foot hung at a weird angle off her leg. She must have been so crazy with anger that she hadn't felt the pain until she tried to stand.

My mother flipped open her cell and dialed 911. It seemed like forever before we heard sirens wailing in the distance.

"I'll go wave them in," Mom said. "So they aren't wandering around the house, looking for the emergency."

"Be care . . . " Callie's words tapered into silence. She had stepped back about ten paces, her arms wrapped around herself even though she wore a hooded sweatshirt.

Everyone in my family responds to stress differently. I

rush around, Mom talks too much, and Dad makes a list. My sister takes the easy way out—she just shuts down. It can take hours or even a day to get her communicating again.

Drives me nuts, but we're supposed to be understanding about it.

Aunt Betty came out of her faint, her face white with pain but her eyes still burning with fury. "Where's my shotgun?" she said.

"Shush," I whispered. "The coyotes are gone."

She squeezed my hand, her head flopping back against my shoulder. I was relieved when the EMTs arrived.

"Mark, you get dressed, get ready to follow the ambulance," Mom said to my father. She turned her attention to the EMTs. "Be careful lifting her. Watch that bad foot, and should I tell you now about her thyroid pills? Or maybe I should run in and get them. And do you need her insurance card? Watch out, because this field is riddled with holes from the goph—"

"Enough!" Aunt Betty yelled with such force that I jumped.

Callie didn't even flinch, just stared as the EMTs carried Aunt Betty to the ambulance. As she drifted toward the house, Mom gave me the *look*.

"Why do I have to go after her?" No one ever runs after me to tell me life doesn't totally suck.

"Just go. Please, Savvy."

I caught up to my sister on the front walk. "Hey, Cal. It's okay. Aunt Betty will get a cast and we can sign it and it'll all be okay. It's just a broken foot, that's all."

She shook her head and walked up the steps.

We met Dad on his way out. As Callie drifted by, I passed the *look* to him.

He shook his head. "I've got to go to the hospital with Aunt Betty. Tell Mom."

"She already knows."

Typical—everyone going in different directions, leaving me to play nanny to the sensitive one. Callie was great when times were great, but at the least bit of trouble, forget the cake and ice cream. It was all about what she needed, and not what she could do to help.

I suppose it wasn't her fault, but I could have lived without the pathetic routine tonight.

Dad crossed the yard to his car. I wandered back to the ambulance. Aunt Betty, pasty under the harsh lights, pointed at me. "Savvy, you know what to do."

"I do? Wait! No, I don't," I said, but the EMT shut the doors.

"What did she mean by that?" I asked my mother.

"She probably thinks you should go back to bed and get some sleep."

"Is that what you're going to do?"

"In a little while."

I rested my chin on the top of Mom's head. "Callie's zoned out. I'm sorry, I couldn't—"

"I'll talk to her. Let's go inside."

The wail of the sirens made me think of the coyotes. The farm, with all its trees, weeds, and bushes offered too many places to hide. They could be watching us right now and we'd never know.

A cold fear leaked into my bones.

"I'll come along in a few minutes," I said.

Mom hugged me and headed back into the house. I vowed to dribble up and down the driveway until I chased that stupid fear back into the night.

CHAPTER FOUR

I spun the basketball on my finger, trying to figure out what Aunt Betty meant when she said *Savvy, you know what to do.*

Did she expect me to patrol the pasture and chase the coyotes away? Chasing predators was Sultana's job. Find her dog, I realized. That's what Aunt Betty wanted me to do. Why didn't she just say it?

"Sultana? Come on, girl. Sul-tan-a!"

The low pasture shone like tinsel in the moonlight. The sheep clustered in the middle of their pen. Like Callie, maybe they also were tight with a fear they couldn't speak aloud.

"Sultana! Come on, girl. Where the heck are you?"

The darkness swallowed my voice. The woods beyond the fence were veiled in shadow, creeping me out. On a moonlit night in the desert you could see forever. Rhode Island might as well be Mars, it was that weird. Every morning the dew was so heavy, it soaked through my sneakers. At dusk or when the sun wasn't out, the mosquitoes were.

And yet, tonight the cool air and bright stars made me feel as big as the night around me. I leaped as high as I could and cupped my hands around both sides of the moon. If I could bring down that rebound, no one in the world would ever steal it back.

I dribbled the moon-ball around the sheep. An old ewe

stepped up to block me, but I jabbed to my right and did a spinning layup over her head. I shot from the far side of the pasture—a three-point swish—and from the far side of the stars, a shot for which no points could be calculated.

A savvy shot, they'd call it. Named after the famous Savannah Christopher. A shot so wonderful that all the coyotes in the world couldn't stuff it.

I raced around the flock, high-fiving my woolly teammates. "Good game, good game, good—"

I tripped over something cold and hard, like a rock. But not a rock.

⊙⊪-⊙⊪-⊙⊪-⊙⊪

"Not a mark on her," Mom said. "She must have had a heart attack. Aunt Betty will be devastated."

"She already knows," I said.

Mom sighed. "I expect you're right. I'm sorry you had to find the dog like this."

"Good thing Callie didn't." Even though my sister wasn't much for animals, she had said more than once that Sultana had good form. As a cheerleader and gymnast, my sister appreciated good form.

When we watch the old videos of Dad golfing, Callie always remarks on how smooth his stroke was. Where she sees grace, I see power. Too bad we never got to see him in real life doing the one thing he loved best.

I was three and Callie was five when *the accident* happened. Dad had climbed onto the roof to adjust our satellite dish after a wind storm. Callie scampered up the ladder after him. Dad was so startled to see her that he slipped on a screwdriver. She watched as he fell two stories to the ground, breaking bones in his neck and his back.

My mother checked her watch. "I have got to get some sleep before work."

"We can't just leave her like this."

"I'll call one of the neighbors in the morning. No, wait. I'm taking the Millipore people out for breakfast. They're my first big account, so I can't mess it up. I'll call around after lunch. See if someone can take care of this for us."

"You don't know any of the neighbors," I said.

"Yeah, there is that, isn't there?" She yawned. "I'll figure something out."

"Maybe I can figure it out for you."

"It's not your problem, sweetie. And you've been out here long enough. Come on in."

Maybe it wasn't my problem, but Dad was at the hospital, Mom's eyes were baggy, and Callie was—well, Callie. Someone had to do something.

"No, you go," I said. "I'll come in soon."

"Savvy, please."

"I'll be fine. You go."

She yawned again and mumbled, "Don't be too long."

I jogged over to the barn. It was packed with junk, including an endless supply of empty feed bags. Rocks would secure the burlap over Sultana's body until someone could do something. Yeah, good plan, I thought, resisting the urge to high-five my shadow.

I stood in the doorway, breathing in ancient wood and damp earth. A bird chirped nearby, starting a chorus of squawks and whistles in the rafters. I turned off the light so I could gaze out at the fields. The sky in the east shaded to gray. The world was waking up.

But the night wasn't over yet. Somewhere in the woods beyond the house, a coyote yapped. A burlap bag and a couple of rocks wouldn't stop them if they came back.

I found a shovel, went back out to the pasture, and started to dig.

CHAPTER FIVE

Pinnies *rock*.

Pinnies mean scrimmage. Scrimmage means competition. Competition on the basketball court makes my blood rush.

After arguing once with Callie about how to spell pinny, she checked her online dictionary. "It's short for pinafore," she said. "Do I have to look that one up for you too?"

"Got it, don't want it," I said.

Pinafores are what girls used to wear in the dark ages before jeans and T-shirts, back when girls danced and curtsied instead of dribbled and shot. Pinafores are what girls wore before we played basketball with the same rules that boys do.

When Coach Fitzgerald brought out the game ball, my heart beat double-time. Maybe I had flopped through some of his drills, but I could compete with anyone in a game situation. He had to see that.

He tossed the first pinny to Molly, the girl with the black braid. A slick shooter, she was going into her sophomore year in high school.

The next pinny went to Bubble. Her real name was Natalie, but Gonzo said the girls called her that because nothing bothered her. She was the only kid on Fire who had gone out of her way to be nice to us.

The third pinny went to Bailey, a skinny girl who could

really battle under the boards. No one could dislodge her from the lane once she Velcro-ed in.

Molly, Bailey, Bubble—Fitz was giving pinnies to girls who would clearly be his starters.

The fourth pinny went to Gonzo. She slid it on over her T-shirt, trying not to grin. I held my breath, hoping and praying that Fitz would look my way. I had to rub my hands together so I wouldn't just snatch that pinny out of his hands.

He tossed it to Shoulders—Lori Penske. "You girls start. Orange bench will be . . ."

Fitz pulled out another pinny, looked at the rest of us.

Christopher, I tried to will into his head. He tossed it to Ava, a girl with chocolate brown hair that she always wore in French braids.

The rest of us were the white team. Olivia—a take-charge girl with incredibly long legs—set our positions. Naturally she put me on the bench for the start of the scrimmage.

I watched glumly as Gonzo tore through the white team's zone like it was smoke. Molly and Bailey were smooth shooters. No way could I prove that I was better while riding the pine.

Ava sat next to me. "This sucks, huh?"

I tried not to double-take at her actually speaking to me. "Yeah. I want out there so bad."

"Don't worry, rookie. Fitz is fair. He'll get us in."

After six minutes, Fitz whistled the bench players in. Before starting play up again, he whispered something to Gonzo. She glanced my way, then nodded.

"What's up?" I mouthed to her, but she pretended not to see me.

Fitz tossed the ball to Ava to start play. She passed in to Gonzo, who dribbled right at me.

"Better move, dude," she said. "I'm coming through you."

"You and what bulldozer?" I faked forward and left, trying to drive her toward Olivia.

Gonzo stopped dead in her tracks. I plowed right into her and she somersaulted backward.

Tweet!

"Offensive on Christopher," Fitz shouted. "Gonzalez, can the acting."

"Drama queen," I said, totally pissed. Fouling after only ten seconds in the scrimmage was a sure way to bottom out on Fitz's depth chart.

Ava took the ball out again. Her eyes flicked left. Behind me, Lori set up to take the pass. I jumped up and *slap!* I knocked the ball out of the air and dribbled away with it. She caught up with me at the top of the zone, then stepped aside so she wouldn't foul.

Gonzo flew at me, driving me to the left of the basket. As I pushed off, I shifted the ball to my right hand. Ready to leap—

—when Gonzo snatched the ball away. She passed down the court to Bailey, who went up from the left side and found the hoop.

Stealing my two points for the pinny team.

O≡-O≡-O≡-O≡-

Our teammates climbed to the top of the bleachers for the break. They formed a tight circle, one we couldn't penetrate. Gonzo wore a smile but a muscle jumped under her ear.

When we biked downtown to shop, she was everyone's best friend, striking up conversations with salespeople and grocery clerks. Miss Congeniality was probably never excluded from anything in her life.

I dug through my bag, trying to find my towel. Lori sneered down on me like she had swallowed a peeled lemon. "That gym bag is disgusting, rookie."

"Why, thank you. It's one of my cherished traditions," I said.

"If you ask me, it's ridiculously infantile. Don't you ever clean it out?"

"What? And disrespect tradition?" The side compartment of my bag was stuffed with last season's dirty socks. We had won the league championship and went on to finish third in the state. When we played our first tournament in a few weeks, I'd wash them all and start a new collection. Each time we won, the lucky socks would go in the pocket unwashed. If we lost, I'd have to scrub the socks by hand— ridding them of bad karma.

Okay, maybe it was a dumb tradition, but all great athletes had them. Is it my fault that my destiny was linked to smelly socks?

"So you never finished telling me," Gonzo said. "Did your aunt get any?"

"Any what?" I shoved a towel up under my shirt to swab down my belly. Apparently it didn't occur to anyone in Rhode Island to air-condition their gyms.

"Coyotes. Did she shoot any?"

"You can't just go around shooting coyotes," Lori said.

"They're protected." For someone who refused to speak to us, the girl sure had a lot to say.

I unwrapped my turkey sandwich, so hungry, I could go termite on the bleachers.

"You're not supposed to eat in the gym," Lori said.

Bite me, I thought, and took my own bite.

"Coyotes are taking over the town," Gonzo said. "My father chased one out of the trash last week. It ran off with the fish heads, like they were just the coolest thing ever."

"My aunt broke her ankle last night, chasing them away from the sheep with her shotgun," I said. "She's in the hospital. And her livestock dog died, so we don't know what to do."

"Your dog died? Oh, how sad," Molly said, her hand to her mouth. The only thing she'd said to me since tryouts was *Get off my foot, you fool.*

Bailey chimed in. "I hate coyotes. They killed our cat. The newspaper said they're coming into the cities and neighborhoods all over the East Coast. And they are not afraid of humans. I hope your aunt drilled the whole lot of 'em with bullets."

"Shotguns have buckshot. Not bullets." Lori dabbed her face with a tissue. "You're making a big thing of nothing. She probably shot into the ground."

"Trust me, she was gunning for them," I said.

"Oh, that is so illegal."

I knew already that Lori was the type who would rather let an opponent swarm her zone than risk committing a foul. Sometimes you've got to claim your turf, even if it does draw a whistle.

I stood up so I could look Lori straight in the eye. "Sometimes you've got to do what it takes, no matter what."

We glared a full ten-count before Gonzo whacked the back of my leg. "What are you going to do?"

"No clue."

"You'd better find out, Christopher. It'll be dark again . . ." Lori pointed up at the clock on the wall. "In six hours."

O＝O＝O＝O＝

Fitz asked to speak to me after practice.

Oh grief, I thought. I can't take another *you're talented but you suck* conversation.

"What's up, Coach?" I said.

"You learn anything at practice today?"

"Yeah. I'm glad Gonzo and Bubble are on my team."

"You think the guards on the teams we play won't be as good as Gonzalez and Muir?"

"I guess . . . I don't know. Being new and all."

When you play on a travel team—whether it's basketball, softball, or even cheerleading—you get to know the competition in your age bracket really well. Year after year, you see each other at scrimmages, tournaments, and qualifiers. Sometimes you become friends. Sometimes you hate each other at first and become friends later.

Sometimes you hate each other forever.

"Let me put this another way," Fitz said. "There was a theme to what I asked Gonzalez and Muir to do. Did you notice, Christopher?"

I studied my sneakers. Only two months old, they were already tight. Like my family's situation. *Tight*. We told everyone back home we had moved to Rhode Island to help Aunt Betty on her farm. A charitable notion, but the truth was we were the ones who needed the handout.

Fitz cleared his throat. "I asked you a question, gal."

I shrugged.

"Come on, Christopher. I saw it in your face every time you tried to get to the basket."

"Gonzo kept driving me left. May I be excused now? My father needs to get home. He's got class tonight."

"Why do you think I asked Gonzalez to stay on you like that?"

Genius that I am, I tossed off another shrug.

"Because you are easy to defend."

My cheeks burned. "I've been the top scorer on every team I ever played on. I can't be *that* easy to defend."

"You here to learn or to tell me how great you are?"

I clicked my jaw shut before I said something I regretted.

"You're nearly unstoppable from the right side of the basket, especially with that great jumper," Fitz said. "But the fact that you overwhelmingly favor your dominant side makes you predictable. And, for a big gal, you're not very strong. That peanut Gonzalez pushed you around the floor like a shopping cart."

My stomach growled. How long would this little one on one last before I died of starvation? Or humiliation.

"There's an old saying in basketball," he said. "'You can coach talent, but you can't coach size.' You got both, Christopher, which is why I took a chance on you. You wanna knock all these older gals aside and start for this team?"

"Yeah. Of course."

"It's yours for the taking. But only if . . ." His dark eyes locked on mine.

I had to ask. "*If* what?"

"If you boost your game."

"I'm doing the stuff you told me to. What more do I have to do?"

Fitz told me. I didn't like what I was hearing.

But I listened anyway.

CHAPTER SIX

We got home from practice to find Mom waiting for us on the front porch. Still dressed in her business suit, she juggled the cordless phone in one hand and her cell in the other.

"What?" Dad asked. They communicate in the same shortened way Gonzo and I instant message.

"The hospital."

"Bad?"

"Potentially."

"What's wrong and what's for supper?" I said. I can't ever seem to eat enough. The growth spurt of the century, Dad calls it.

"Callie will fill you in." My mother went on to fill me in, of course, because she can't help herself. She talks for a living, could sell slime to a slug.

A bunch of blood clots from Aunt Betty's leg had traveled to her lungs. The doctors wanted my parents in on the conversation about busting them up. Apparently my father's aunt wasn't being too cooperative.

Dad beeped the horn. "Come on, Terri. Let's go!"

Mom handed me the phone. "Order takeout. Ask your sister what she wants."

They drove off and I went inside. Because my aunt was so outdoorsy, her house was not much to look at. The wallpaper was about fifty years old, a faded flowery print. The rooms were filled with overstuffed furniture that smelled like ancient history.

Our house in New Mexico had six bedrooms, four bathrooms, an inground pool, and a hot tub. My parents bought it when Dad was still on the PGA tour. After the accident, he tried to resume his career. Each year he slipped further out of the money and deeper into pain. The back and neck surgery put an end to most of his physical suffering, but he would never swing a golf club again.

My parents made happy blah-blah about Rhode Island being an opportunity to start over. Nice story, but the truth was that we went bankrupt. At the same time, my grandfather decided that his older sister shouldn't live alone anymore. The plan was that Dad would go to college in Providence while we lived with Aunt Betty on her farm.

Aunt Betty converted the dining room into her bedroom so my family could have the whole upstairs to ourselves. Two bedrooms and one creaky bathroom were a tight fit for a family used to a six-bedroom house. The bedroom Callie and I shared was about the same size as our walk-in closets back home.

I found Callie on the top bunk, plugged into her iPod. Her zone of privacy, she calls it. She has more zone schemes than the Phoenix Suns. Mom kept telling her to go outside, get some exercise. The most my sister said in return was, "I'm not a little kid. Don't tell me to go outside and play."

We were all counting the days until Callie's cheerleading practice started. She'd been a silent lump for almost a month now, pouting over leaving New Mexico. I hated moving cross-country too, but no one seemed much concerned about my mood.

I tickled the bottom of her foot. "Hey."

She jumped a mile. "What?"

"What do you want for supper? We're supposed to order out."

"The usual," she said.

"One large sausage and mushroom pizza, two chef salads on the way."

"Savvy, wait. I'm starved," Callie said. "Order two pizzas."

I squinted at her. She had her hand in a bag of cheese puffs. Her teeth and lips were orange.

She glared at me. "You're not the only one who gets hungry."

I was halfway out the door when something occurred to me. "Hey. What're you wearing?"

Without bothering to answer, Callie rolled over to face the wall. The label on the back of her jeans confirmed my suspicion.

"Those are mine," I said. "Give them back."

"They don't fit you anymore."

Callie had me there. I had outgrown all my jeans in May. My parents said I should wear shorts all summer—their budget couldn't keep up with buying me new jeans every two weeks.

"I don't care. I want them back. And who said you could cut off the legs?" Callie had made short-shorts out of my jeans, with a fancy, hand-sewn hem. Nice for her she had plenty of time to screw with my stuff.

She fiddled with her iPod, turning it so loud, I could hear music coming from her earbuds.

I dragged her off the top bunk, thinking I'd take my jeans right off her. She squealed and slapped, but even if Callie wanted to really fight back, she couldn't—not with me towering almost a foot over her. With the same thick brown hair and pale hazel eyes, I was the super-sized freak version of my sister.

Suddenly this was all too weird and I let her go.

"Just ask before you go destroying someone else's property," I said.

"Yeah, whatever." She nodded and climbed back up onto the bed.

I slammed the door on my way out. It didn't occur to me until much later to wonder why jeans that were two sizes too big for my older but much tinier sister suddenly fit her so well.

CHAPTER SEVEN

Callie came down from her self-imposed exile to eat pizza and watch the National Cheerleading Competition with me. Her team had gone to regionals two years ago. They had almost made it high enough in the bracket to get on television.

"This place sucks," Callie said.

I was in no mood for nanny duty, so I grabbed another piece of pizza and shoveled it down.

Callie wasn't about to let it go. "How'd you get over it so fast?"

I shrugged. "I got basketball. When your cheerleading starts, it won't be so bad."

"Yeah. I guess."

The phone rang. Callie grabbed it, listened, and rubbed her forehead.

"What?" I said.

"Mom. Calling from . . . you know." Even saying the word *hospital* freaks her out.

I sighed, reached for the phone.

"No. I'll . . . take this." Callie swiped her hand over her face, spoke into the phone. "When are you coming home?"

I waved at her, trying to figure out what was going on. She held up an index finger to tell me to wait. For once, she was trying—I'd give her that.

"Yeah, we'll be all right," she said, and hung up the phone.

"What's going on?"

"There's a big clot lodged in the vein near Aunt Betty's heart. They're trying to dissolve it with some dangerous medicine that makes all your blood really, really slippery. Like if you nicked her finger, it wouldn't stop bleeding."

I rolled my eyes. "I learned about platelets in science last year."

"Aunt Betty keeps telling them to go home but . . ." She took a long breath, exhaled in little puffs.

"But what?"

"Dad said we're her family and we're going to act like it. Mom wanted you to call over to the Gonzalezes' house about us staying there overnight. I said no, that we'd be okay here until they got home. Right?"

"Yeah. Course."

"Even if it's all night?"

"I said yeah. Sheesh, Cal. We're not babies."

Callie rubbed her arms. "What about the coyotes?"

Without a livestock guardian dog or gun-toting lady, the coyotes would have a clear lane for the sheep. The big ones could fend them off, but there were all those spring lambs, only half-grown and out there for the taking.

"We need to go check on them," I said. "Okay?"

"It's dark out."

"So? We'll use flashlights."

"I can't step in a hole, break my ankle. Not with cheerleading about to start."

"Like I can? We'll do it carefully. Okay?"

"All right," she said. "But just so you know, if I see a slug, I am so out of there."

I whirled away and did a pretend jump shot. I didn't want her to read what I was thinking. At least you could stomp the life out of slugs. I had no clue what we would do about those coyotes.

Callie did have an idea, however. A real three-pointer.

○=○=○=○=

Bam! Bam! Something battered the front door, waking me out of a dead sleep.

I shook Callie. "Someone's trying to break into the house."

Bam! Bam!

She sat up, the moonlight turning her face to ice. Slowly, slowly, she pulled the blanket over her head.

"No," I said, ripping it away. "I need your help."

We slipped out into the front hall, each *bam* sending shock waves through both of us. Callie grabbed the back of my T-shirt and we crept toward the top of the stairs. Too bad I didn't play softball—at least then I'd have a bat for a weapon. Callie's pom-poms and my WNBA basketball were no match for whatever was trying to bust our door down.

We dropped to our bellies at the top of the stairs, trying to see through the little windows over the front door.

Bam! Bam!

"Call 911," Callie whispered.

"Wait. Look." Red and blue lights flashed through the trees. "911 is already here."

"What are the cops . . . ?" My sister's breath caught in her throat.

"Don't go there," I said, though how could we not? Middle of the night, police pounding the door meant bad news.

Losing our home would be nothing compared to losing our parents.

I slid my arm around Callie's shoulders. "We've got to see what they want."

"No. If we just keep quiet, they'll go away."

I grabbed her wrist. "I'm going downstairs and you're coming with me."

We slid down the steps, trying to keep out of sight. Lowering my voice to sound older, I called out: "Who's there?"

"Police. We've had a complaint. Open up, ma'am." A rusty voice—the guy must smoke a thousand cigarettes a day.

"Savvy . . ." Callie would sink through the floor if I didn't hold her up.

"Show me a badge," I shouted.

Clink! The guy pressed something against the glass. It appeared real, but how could we know? He could have gotten it at a costume shop.

I let go of Callie and grabbed an umbrella from the hall closet. She crept partway up the stairs. "You stay here with me," I said.

Her face went blank.

"I swear, I'll smack you with this umbrella if you don't stay with me."

She grabbed my arm and hung on tight.

Bam, bam! "Open up!"

I unlocked the door and opened it. A baggy-eyed, tight-mouthed cop stood on the front porch. He smirked at the umbrella and said, "Your parents home?"

"Thank God," Callie whispered. If this guy was asking about Mom and Dad, then he couldn't be here to deliver bad news about them.

"No," I said. "They're at the hospital. My father's aunt is very sick."

"Miss Christopher is ailing, huh? Then you should be very ashamed," Rusty said.

"Huh?"

"Parents away, aunt sick, and you girls are partying. Disgusting."

"What are you talking about?" Callie said. "You woke us up from a sound sleep."

Rusty stepped out onto the front porch and pointed out toward the pasture. "So it's the sheep that are having that party?"

Callie had set a boom box at full blast between the pasture and the woods. She had burned a CD, figuring that the music that drove our parents crazy would drive the coyotes away.

"Sorry, officer," I said. "It was an emergency. Our dog died and we need to scare off the coyotes."

"What, the coyote-ate-our-homework excuse? Good one, girls."

I smiled to show there were no hard feelings.

Rusty stepped close, looked up at me. "Go turn that thing off and send your friends home before I take the bunch of you down to the station."

"We don't have any friends," I said. "Only the sheep."

"Kid, you think I fell off the turnip truck? No adults around, music cranked up, your pals scattered in the woods somewhere? That's party time in my book. Justice will be served when they get covered with mosquito bites and poison ivy."

"But what about the sheep?"

"I swear, kid, you're one *but* away from getting hauled down to the station. Get out there and turn off that noise. Now!"

"Yes sir, right away," I said.

Rusty got in his cruiser and watched while I slogged out to the pasture and grabbed the boom box. On my way back to the house, he motioned me over.

"Someone your age should set a better example for her little sister. Shame on you."

"But . . ." Why bother explaining? I just mumbled *yes sir*.

"Hope your party pals all get the poison ivy they deserve," he yelled as he drove off.

I went inside, expecting to find Callie huddled under her covers. Instead, she was in the kitchen, plowing through a giant bowl of vanilla ice cream and chocolate sauce. "Stupid neighbors. People should mind their own business," she said. "Want some?"

"No." My stomach was tied in a knot from fear, anger, and now the realization that the pasture had just become an all-night supermarket for the coyotes.

AUGUST

CHAPTER EIGHT

When August rolled around, Aunt Betty was still in the hospital. She had caught pneumonia, her leg got infected, and she had another surgery to remove the pins in her ankle. Aunt Betty refused to see anyone but my parents.

I spent half my time trying to follow the elaborate plan Fitz had set out to boost my game and the other half trying to keep the sheep safe. Dad said Aunt Betty didn't seem to care much. I'm not sure why I did—maybe it was for the same reason I had to make the 18s.

I can't resist a challenge.

Gonzo said we should pee around the boundary of the woods to repel the coyotes. "Mark our territory," she said. "Like dogs."

"You go right ahead," I said, and of course, she did.

Dad and I strung electrified wire around both pastures. I did the heavy lifting while he supplied the brain power.

The coyotes dug under the wire and we lost two more lambs. Finally I just herded the sheep into the barn every night and cleaned out all the poop every morning.

Mom said I didn't have to do any of this, but someone had to do something. Callie slept with her iPod on every night so she didn't have to hear the pack running in the woods, screeching after prey.

Nature's way, my father said, but I couldn't bear the

coyotes circling around our property, looking for something to devour. Shoveling poop stunk, but herding sheep was kind of fun.

"What does Aunt Betty suggest we do?" I had asked my father.

He sighed and said, "She won't talk about it. Won't talk about much, I'm afraid."

Maybe I inherited the Christopher height, but we could blame Aunt Betty for Callie's silent act.

O⹀O⹀O⹀O⹀

We all cheered when my sister's first high school practice arrived. She'd been bizarre the whole week before, spending every day locked in our room and practicing her New Mexico routines. Totally stupid because the high school team would have their own unique routines and it wasn't like she could actually tumble or jump in a room the size of a doghouse.

Mom said she was visualizing success and I should give Callie her space.

Callie and I had practice the same day that week. Fire started an hour earlier, in the high school's small gym. Figures—cheerleaders got all the good stuff.

The plan was for Gonzo and me to wait for Callie so Dad could pick us all up on his way home from college. Gonzo and I were heading for the other gym after practice to watch some of the cheering when she detoured us to the left.

"Where are we going?" I asked.

"The cheerleaders aren't the only ones who began practice today."

"What do you mean?"

Gonzo grinned. "You'll see."

At the end of the hall was the school's weight room. My knees noodled when I looked inside and saw big guys working hard to get bigger. "Is that the football team?"

"Yeah, baby. There ought to be a law against them lifting weights without shirts. Those pecs and abs luring sweet little girls like me—"

I laughed. "Little, maybe. Sweet? Not so much."

"Which one do you think is the hottest?"

"I don't know."

"Okay," Gonzo said. "The coolest, then. Make your pick."

For me, the qualifying factor was not hottest or coolest. It was tallest. One goofy kid with spiked hair looked about six five. He had to weigh three hundred pounds, most of it flab. Another kid had to be six eight, but he was all cheekbones and knobby knees—probably a cross-country runner mixed in with the big guys.

Then I spotted a heart-slammin' guy with black hair and amazing shoulders. Six one, maybe even taller. He looked our way and smiled, melting me like a Popsicle on hot pavement.

"Ah. That's Marc Sardakis. Wide receiver," Gonzo said. "Smokin', huh?"

It should be illegal for a guy that good-looking to have eyes that blue. And even this far away, I could see his long, dark lashes.

Some guy in glasses and street clothes pushed through the door. He did a double take when he saw me—the *how tall is that girl, is she some kind of freak* look.

The heat in my belly turned to a lump of cement. I spun away, headed for the gym. "We gotta go get Callie."

Gonzo trotted after me. "Hey, it's early. What's up?"

"Nothing."

"Come on, girl. Dish."

"Nothing."

She grabbed my T-shirt, yanked me to a stop. "Something. Speak it."

I sighed. "Don't you know *the* rule?"

"Oh please. That football-players-only-dating-cheerleaders thing is so old-school."

"Not that rule."

"Which rule, then?"

I looked her square in the eye. "The rule that guys have to date girls shorter than them. Which disqualifies me from almost the whole human race."

She stood there—for once in her life—with absolutely nothing to say.

O═O═O═O═

Some people call cheering a sport. Others say it's an art form. Callie loves cheering because it's structured. She doesn't mind getting thrown up in the air because she knows exactly where her teammates will be when she comes back down.

My parents put me in cheering when I was six. When they found out I spent every practice shooting my pom-poms at imaginary baskets instead of shaking them for imaginary football players, they let me switch.

Basketball is chaos with a rule book. Unlike cheering,

there's no way to predict where the ball—or you—will land. You can run all the plays in the world, but you have no control over what your opponent will throw at you. I love the game because every dribble, shot, or pass is an opportunity for disaster or glory.

Gonzo and I watched Callie practice from the top of the bleachers. We both understood this was an important day for her. She would be starting high school in a month as the new kid. The best way to fit in was the one thing she did well—be a cute cheerleader.

The squad tumbled through a simple routine, crossing in backflips and ending in splits. Four girls formed a base and lifted Callie over their heads. She balanced on one leg and stretched the other over her head. An expert gymnast, she could do this stunt in her sleep.

It happened in a snap, but I watched it unfold in slow motion.

Callie's knees wobbling—her base team staggering—Callie pitching sideways—Gonzo gasping—my heart somersaulting—a spotter reaching for her—Callie toppling.

She landed elbow first with a loud crack.

I leaped to my feet, praying she was okay. A knot of girls clustered around her.

"It's okay, I'm fine," she said.

Ms. Kubek, the cheerleading coach, checked Callie's arm. When she was convinced nothing was broken, she made Callie sit on the bottom bleacher with ice pressed to her elbow. I waved and smiled encouragement.

Callie slumped on the bench and stared at her feet.

After practice, the squad went into the locker room to shower and change. Gonzo and I went outside to the town courts and shot baskets for a while. Dad drove up, grumbled at us. "Go find your sister. See if she's going to be ready to leave any time this millennium."

We went back in, heard Callie was in the office talking with Ms. Kubek. Gonzo and I looked at each other, and decided—without a word—to listen.

"I don't understand," Callie was saying.

"It appears that you've put on weight since tryouts."

Callie sighed. "Maybe a little."

Ms. Kubek sighed with her. "You are not the . . . um . . . petite girl we saw at tryouts. And you seem to have lost some strength as well. The stunts you did two months ago were very impressive, but now . . ."

She didn't have to finish the sentence. Anyone who had seen the practice knew my sister was flabby and out of shape.

"I got a little behind on my conditioning," Callie said.

I exhaled loudly, didn't even realize I had been holding my breath. Gonzo waved at me to be quiet.

Ms. Kubek cleared her throat. Never a good sign when adults clear their throats. "The thing is, Callie, you could have broken your arm when you fell. Or worse."

"Water weight," Callie said. "It'll be gone by next week."

"Water weight. Hm."

A sigh, a throat clearing, and a *hm*. Not good.

"Yes. Water weight." My sister sounded stronger, like she believed the garbage she was selling.

"Do you normally retain this much water?"

Trick question. What Ms. Kubek really asked was: "Will you be too heavy to fly one week out of every four?"

"We had Chinese food last night and the night before we had . . . um . . . hot dogs. And mac and cheese. All that salt, two nights in a row. Bad, bad timing."

Liar—we had chicken and baked potatoes last night, spaghetti two nights ago.

"You're what—fifteen, right?" Ms. Kubek said. "If you're still growing, we can make adjustments—"

"Wait. What adjustments?" The panic in Callie's voice was painful.

"If the weight doesn't come off—and hear me when I say *it's okay* if it doesn't—we can move you to the reserve roster. You practice with the team and when a base position opens up, you can take that. But for now, please eat healthy and just get some exercise. Consider doing some weight training to get your strength back. Okay?"

"Water weight," Callie said. "I swear that's all it is."

A chair scraped along the floor. We booked it down the hall.

"It's not water weight. Is it?" Gonzo asked. She had seen the trash in our room from potato chips, Twinkies, cookies, peanut butter cups, cheese and crackers, soda.

But family had to stick together—no matter how annoying.

"Sure," I said. "Water weight. It'll be gone before you know it."

CHAPTER NINE

Supper was beef stew. Callie piled on the salad but only picked at her stew. After a few minutes, she pushed away from the table. "I'm done."

"You barely touched your dinner," Dad said. "Not hungry?"

"I am." I grabbed the corn bread off Callie's plate. An awesome cook, my father should forget this business school nonsense and open a restaurant.

"It's not fair." Callie blinked back tears.

Sheesh—the girl's upset because I took the bread she didn't want? "What's not fair?" I said.

"You."

"What're you talking about?"

"The whole superstar thing. Everything comes easy for you." Callie ran out of the kitchen.

"What was that all about?" my father said. "Is she okay?"

As usual, this was all about Callie. Which meant, if I told him what Ms. Kubek said, I'd get busted for eavesdropping worse than she would for oinkin' out all summer.

I stood, cleared my dishes and my sister's. "I gotta go move the sheep."

"Go relax or shoot some baskets. I'll do it."

The bags under my father's eyes were almost as puffy as his knapsack. He was taking two summer courses, which meant twelve hours of class, plus countless of homework.

Sitting down all that time was painful, and the drive back and forth to Providence didn't help. He never complained, but he downed a lot of ibuprofen and always seemed to have an ice pack on his back or neck.

"I like doing it," I said.

"You shouldn't have to do it every night. I'll tell Callie to help you."

Herding the sheep was peaceful. Callie picking through the pasture, worried about snakes and slugs, would be tortuous.

"No, I want to do it."

The phone rang. Dad answered it. He listened for a minute, saying *uh-huh* every once in a while. He hung up and turned to me. "Aunt Betty's back in intensive care."

"More blood clots?"

"A bad infection. She's delirious. Mom wants me to get there ASAP." He grabbed his keys and left.

I had just slipped on Aunt Betty's field boots and was ready to head out when the doorbell rang. It was one of the cheerleaders, a blond girl with those peachy-clear cheeks old ladies love to tweak. She wore short-shorts and a halter top.

If you've got it, make sure people see it, I guess.

"Is Callie home?" she said.

"Yeah. Um . . . come on in."

She extended her hand. "I'm Alyssa Bouchard."

I'd never shaken hands with a kid before. "I'm Savvy. Callie's sister."

Alyssa looked me up and down. Uh-oh. Here comes the

how tall are you. Or maybe she'd ask if I always wore rubber boots in the house.

She surprised—shocked—me when she asked, "Do you model?"

"Me?"

"Yeah. I tried to get in with an agency last year but they said I was too fat. So I'm working out a bunch, trying to get my BMI down."

"Huh?" I sounded as bright as a fungus.

"Body Mass Index. Also known as *flab*. The camera goes right to mine, especially because I'm so short."

Short? The girl had to be five nine. And if this girl was fat, Callie was a flippin' walrus. Had Ms. Kubek sent this girl to bust my sister about her BMI?

Alyssa chattered on. "You'd be perfect, Savvy. So tall and thin. And the camera would love your cheekbones. I'll give you the number of the agency in Boston, if you want to call them."

"Um . . . thanks. But I'm kinda into basketball right now."

"Cool. But if you change your mind, just let me know." She nodded at the stairs. "Should I just go up?"

"I think Callie's sleeping."

Alyssa touched my arm. "Poor girl had a tough day at practice. I just want to make sure she's all right."

"Okay. Um . . . let me go check."

I found Callie in the closet, her hand in her mouth and her head over the wastebasket.

"You are so not making yourself throw up!" I said.

56

"Go use the bathroom if you're going to go bulimic on yourself."

Callie kicked the wastebasket aside and launched up to the top bunk. "Don't be stupid. My stomach's upset. What do you want, Savvy?"

"Some girl wants to see you. Her name's Alyssa."

"Alyssa? Like, with blond hair and all that?"

"Yeah. All that."

"Really cute?"

"I guess." Like I didn't know.

"Tall? And perfect makeup?"

"Sheesh, Callie. Just go downstairs and see if it's your Alyssa or someone escaped from *America's Most Wanted*."

"I can't see her." Callie rolled over and faced the wall. "Tell her I'm sick and she has to go away."

I climbed up next to her. "Is she here because of what your coach said today?"

"Oh God, take me now," she moaned. "You heard that?"

Callie had always been one big muscle, but as I patted her back, my fingers dug into soft tissue. I climbed between her and the wall, trying to put on my best Tyra Banks act. "You're just out of shape. You can work through this. Exercise more. Tell Mom to buy like, more carrots and broccoli or something when she goes shopping."

"Ohmigosh. Don't tell Mom anything. She'll be all over me until she fixes me."

"You'll fix it. I know you can. Just eat better, work out a bit, Cal." I sat up, my head clunking the ceiling.

She sat with me, arms wrapped around her knees. "Yeah,

I'll do that. But Sav, you've got to swear you won't say anything."

Dad sweated out his college classes and Mom worked hard hours. Poor Aunt Betty struggled to survive. Even the sheep had it bad, the coyotes howling in the woods every night. Snitching about my sister's weight might just add to everyone's stress.

"If you swear you won't do anything stupid, I won't say anything," I said.

Callie put her hand to her heart, then extended it to me, palm out. "I swear."

I touched my heart and then pressed my hand to hers. "I swear."

She gave me a weak smile. "I'm sorry. I didn't mean the whole superstar thing. I mean, you are a superstar. But that's cool with me."

"Glad it's cool with someone, because it's not with my teammates." I waited for a little sympathy to come my way, wasn't surprised that it didn't.

"That Alyssa seems really nice," I said.

"She's the most popular girl in school."

"How do you know that? You haven't even started school."

"Savvy, some things are just obvious."

"So I guess you'd better get down there."

Callie sniffed, wiped her tears on her pillow. "I can't."

I jumped off the bed and tossed her makeup bag at her. "You can't just snub the most popular girl in school."

"I can't do this, Savvy. I just can't."

"Yeah, you can. I'll just hang around until you feel comfortable. Or—here's a better idea. I'll hang around, be kinda stupid, and you can yell at me and throw me out. You and Alyssa can make fun of me later. Okay?"

"Savvy?" Alyssa called from the bottom of the stairs. "Is Callie awake? Can I come up?"

"She's gonna think something is really weird in about ten seconds if I don't answer her."

"Okay," she said, brushing foundation under her eyes to hide the redness. "Just don't act like too big a jerk."

"It'll be hard. But I'll try not to."

CHAPTER TEN

A couple days later, Gonzo and I had an hour to kill after practice. Some of our teammates headed for the stone wall in front of the high school where they cooled off before going home. Stupid us, we followed them there.

Gonzo sat down next to Bailey and got glared at. I knew better than to even try. Our teammates treated us like warts, shooting acid comments whenever we tried to join the conversation. This whole cold-shoulder thing got old fast. Fire was all about being the best, not being a social club.

"Let's shoot hoops," I said. The outdoor courts were empty in the afternoon heat.

Gonzo laughed. "You never stop, do you?"

Easy for her to say. She was on the pinny team.

We were five minutes into a game of HORSE when Gonzo hissed, "Yo, Sav. Get out the fire extinguisher. Look who's coming."

Marc Sardakis and a couple other kids crossed the adjacent court, heading our way.

My tank top was soaked through with sweat and stained with lime sports drink. My hair was knotted on top of my head, making me look two inches taller that I already was. After a hard practice, I stunk like the inside of a trash can.

"Ignore them and keep shooting," I said. "They're just passing by."

"You don't know that. Maybe they're coming to see us."

"Yeah, and maybe the sun will turn into the moon."

Gonzo bricked one from the left side of the key, deliberately trying to rebound the ball toward them. I dove for it and then, embarrassed because I looked like I was showing off, I heaved it from about four feet outside the three-point line.

When I actually made the shot, my skin flamed red. Like I wanted Marc and his friends to notice me? Maybe if I were as short as Gonzo or as perfect as Alyssa, but not like this, looking like some coyote dragged me out of a compost pile.

I passed the ball to Gonzo, almost taking her head off. "Your shot. From here."

Gonzo toed up to the place I had hit from. "This is halfway to New York. I don't have your spider arms," she said. "Besides, that was a panic shot."

"Chicken."

"Shut up. You couldn't make it again."

"You think?"

"If you can, I'll buy you a pizza," Gonzo said.

"Large?"

"Small."

"No way. This is a large-pizza shot."

Marc and his friends stood at half-court, watching us. My back was to them, but their presence—his presence—beat down on my neck like the hot sun.

Gonzo continued the negotiation. "Medium."

"With toppings?"

"Cheese."

"Sausage and mushrooms," I said.

"Too expensive."

"Forget it, then. Take your shot or I win, Gonz."

She bit her lip, her eyeballs practically rolling into her left ear as she tried to look behind us—without actually looking. I burst out laughing. She had tried to macho me into trying to repeat the shot because she didn't want to attempt it with Marc around.

"Sausage," she said. "That's all I can afford."

"You are such a chicken."

"I'll bet a large pizza." I didn't have to turn around to know who had said it.

Gonzo smirked at me, turned to Marc. "Hey man, is that with toppings?"

"As many as you want." Marc looked my way. "Think you can do it again, Hotshot?"

As I tried to cough up a response, Olivia appeared. "Of course she can. She's the best shooter on our team."

Gonzo shot her a filthy look. Now that the hottest guy in the world was talking to us, Olivia was our bff. The rest of the girls watched from the stone wall.

"I've been watching you, Hotshot," Marc said. "You're good. Really good. But are you good enough to repeat a shot? That's where *game* comes in."

Bailey trotted toward us, giving me a finger-wiggle. Where was she during our bathroom break when I asked her to pass me some toilet tissue? Her only response was to flush and slam the door on her way out.

Suddenly I was so pissed, I thought my eyes would explode. I pushed Gonzo off the spot, bounced the ball once, and let it fly.

Swish.

O=O=O=O=

The whole thing turned into a circus, with me as the clown.

Marc's friends doubled-down on a new wager. If he sunk the shot, we'd have to buy them two pizzas.

Of course he netted it because he was so freakin' wonderful. "Let's pay up and go," I whispered to Gonzo.

"No, no!" Bailey said. "Olivia and I will bet three pizzas that Savvy can beat Marc in a game of HORSE."

"I'm in," Gonzo said. "She wins, you guys buy for us. He wins, we buy."

"No," I said. "I can't. I've got to get home."

"Chill. My mom's not due for another forty-five minutes," Gonzo said. "Enough time to wipe the court with him and eat our pizzas."

"Savvy's the best," Olivia said, batting her eyelashes at Marc. In the two hundred feet between the rock wall and the court, she had managed to wipe off her sweat and put on lip gloss.

Marc ignored her, turned his steel-blues on me. "Let's do it, Hotshot. It'll be fun. You first."

I took the ball to the free throw line. Just me and the hoop. Oh yeah, and the rest of my teammates, who had come to the sidelines to cheer me on—girls who wanted me dead ten minutes ago.

Marc stood a few feet to my left. His black hair, long on top, caught the afternoon sun like a halo. The sleeves were ripped off his T-shirt, showing muscular shoulders and biceps.

What would it feel like to have those arms wrapped around me? Come on, fool, I told myself. Focus. Me, the ball, the basket. Simple shot from the free throw line.

I shot and missed.

Marc's friends—the fat kid with the spiked hair and a red-haired kid with braces and a bad sunburn—laughed and high-fived. Marc gave them a dirty look, then wiggled his fingers at me for the ball. He stepped to the left block and hooked one. A rim-rattler that didn't have a chance of going in.

Marc had missed on purpose. He had shown me the ultimate respect of wanting me to sink the first shot so he could match it. The kid was scalding hot *and* a gentleman.

Gonzo tossed me the ball. I chewed my fingernails and tried to lower my heartbeat to a rattle instead of a roar.

I went to the corner and drained my favorite shot. I stayed on the spot until Marc got in position. His foot brushed mine as he toed up. With intense eyes and lips pressed together, he made the shot.

Game on.

After fifteen minutes, we both had HORS. I got him on two three-pointers, one hook, and a corner shot from the right side. He got me on a spinning layup, a backward free throw, a straight-on three, and a high arcing shot from the back side of the basket.

My biggest fear was that he'd try to blast one from full court. Fitz was right—for my size, I wasn't very strong. Even a shot from half-court might kill me. I could heave the ball but wouldn't have the strength to make it fly.

Marc dribbled around the court, examining various angles as he tried to come up with a shot that would put me away. If he missed this shot, I'd be back in control of the ball.

He had to know I'd go straight for my favorite corner. He got lucky once and missed once.

"What to do, what to do," he mumbled. Spike and Red called out suggestions while Olivia and Bailey shoved them and giggled like chickens.

Lori stood behind everyone, wearing her lemon face. "Hey," she called out.

He glanced over at her. She raised her left hand and made a layup motion. He wrinkled his nose. "That's too easy."

"Not for her," she said. "Trust me."

"What're you doing?" Olivia snapped.

"She's the shooting star," Lori said. "She should be able to hit a simple shot."

Marc dribbled three times, leaped, and did a simple left-handed layup.

I'd practiced this over and over for weeks now. I dribbled, leaped, and felt my arms and legs snarl.

The ball slammed off the rim so hard, it caught Marc on the side of the head. He laughed, tossed it at me. "Hey, Hotshot," he said. "You just got HORSEd."

Lori gave a little laugh and walked away.

Maybe my left hand wasn't good enough to shoot with, but I sure as heck could strangle Lori with it.

⊙▬⊙▬⊙▬⊙▬

We hiked in a group to the pizza shop. Marc walked briskly but couldn't get away from Olivia. She buzzed him like a mosquito—any minute I expected him to slap at her.

I fell back, trying to air out my sweat. Bailey slowed down to walk with me. "Hey thanks, Savvy."

"For what? I lost."

She laughed. "Rookie, we're having pizza with Marc Sardakis. Who cares who's paying?"

"If I could have gotten him to the corner one more time, I might have had him."

"About that corner shot," Bailey said. "How do you make it so consistently?"

Finally. Someone on Fire wanted to talk basketball with me. "Letting the backboard into your line of sight will kill you every time because it'll put your shot off-center. If you train yourself just to look at the hoop, you'll hit center rim and not board."

"Wow, okay. So how come you're such a good shooter, Savvy?"

"My father was a professional athlete."

"He played basketball?"

"No, golf. At six one, he was the shortest of his brothers. They all played college ball and my uncle Nate played some pro ball in Europe. His uncles and even his aunt are way over six feet tall."

"Genetic, then. That won't help me. My father doesn't top six feet even. And my mother is a peanut."

"It's not just that," I said. "The thing is, I'm kinda nuts. For as long as I can remember, I had to have a basketball in my hands. I'd shoot hoops waiting for the school bus, shoot them again when I got dropped off, even before I went inside the house. My sister says I'm obsessive-compulsive about it."

"Well, it works for you. And that's cool."

"I can't move the ball like you, though. I'd be a better player if I could. Lori's always sniping at me about handling the ball better. I can't believe how good you are at that."

She smiled at that. "Yeah. I am."

Finally, I thought.

○─○─○─○

Pizza was a stupid waste of time.

Olivia, Gonzo, and Bailey ended up in the booth with the guys.

Savvy, over here, Gonzo mouthed as I came out of the restroom. Even though I had toweled down the best I could, I stunk. I waved my hand under my armpit, indicating my situation.

I slid into the next booth, dabbed my face with a napkin, and prayed I would finally stop pouring sweat. Marc got up, came to me. "Hotshot. Pizza's over here."

"I'm . . . um . . . hot and sweaty. I didn't want to stink you guys out."

He sniffed my neck, touching the tip of his nose to my skin. I thought my bones would melt. "Nah, you're no worse than any of the rest of us. Come on."

67

Marc dragged two chairs over to the booth. I plopped down in one, trying to look cool even though my blood was molten. He put a super-sized cola in front of me. "I bought you a drink."

"I thought . . . uh . . . we were buying for you guys."

"No way. Not you, at least. You and I are the thoroughbreds. They bet on us, they gotta feed us. Right?"

I gulped the soda down too fast and badly needed to burp. I held it back so long, I thought my eardrums would pop. "Excuse me for a sec," I said, and went out to the sidewalk. The burp was so vigorous, I swear the windows rattled.

Gonzo would have just let it go at the table, and made everyone laugh. It's cute when a short girl does something like that. When someone my size does it, it's gross.

Marc came out after me. "Hey, sorry to bust early, but I have to go pick up my sister from babysitting. You going back in? The pizza's just arriving."

"Um . . . yeah. I just needed to cool off some more."

"You play hard, don't you?"

"Yeah. I guess. So do you." My face steamed now from this different kind of game, one I had no clue about playing.

Marc leaned close to me, eye to eye because—bless his heart-stopping self—he was just my height. He put his mouth to my ear and whispered, "Next time, Hotshot."

CHAPTER ELEVEN

A half hour later, Mrs. Gonzalez dropped me off at home.

Callie was at the gym—Alyssa took her every day to work out and lift weights. Mom was still at work, and Dad had school. I had the house to myself.

I ran upstairs, took Fitz's list out of my bag, and tossed my bag into the closet. The shower would come later. According to my coach's worksheet, I still had a ton of basketball practice ahead of me. But first I had to get something to eat. I hadn't been able down a single bite of pizza earlier. Now I'd kill for a grilled cheese sandwich, a mug of tomato soup, and a big glass of ice-cold milk.

I headed for the kitchen, dreaming about Marc's *next time*. I stopped, gasped. Someone had left a skeleton in the living room. Oh God, not a skeleton.

Aunt Betty was home from the hospital.

She sat alone, staring out the bay window. She hadn't let Callie or me visit the whole time she was in there, said she wanted peace and quiet. Clearly, she just didn't want us to see her like this.

A broken ankle, a bunch of blood clots, and an infection had reduced a strong woman to a paper-thin shell. She had a cast up to her knee. Black and blue patches mottled her arms. Her shoulders slumped and her breathing wheezed.

Stupid coyotes.

I was about to creep outside when my stomach growled.

Aunt Betty kept her gaze out the window. "Good afternoon, Savannah."

"Um . . . hi, Aunt Betty. What're you doing here?"

"I live here."

"Yeah. Sorry. Welcome home. I . . . ah . . . was just about going to get something to eat. Can I get you something?"

"No. Thank you."

Dad had left me a note in the kitchen. *Aunt Betty's home—* no foolin'—*so if the visiting nurse comes, let her in. Be polite, and helpful.*

I prayed the nurse would get her butt here before Aunt Betty keeled over and left me picking up the bones. I hated myself for this whole night-of-the-living-dead attitude but sheesh, Dad should have warned me she was coming home today.

I made my grilled cheese, cut it in four pieces, and took two out to Aunt Betty. "Have some."

"No, thank you."

"You sure? I made it with double cheese."

"Go play, Savannah. I'm all right."

Back in the kitchen, I gulped down my sandwich without tasting it. Rather than pass by Aunt Betty again, I escaped out the back door.

Fitz had been a miserable jerk at practice, torqued because I dribbled in for my left-side layup with my right hand. Talk about child abuse—he made me wear a mitten on my right hand during scrimmage.

Lori had a lot of nerve, cueing Marc to my weak side.

The heck with them. I grabbed my basketball and did fifty or sixty layups from the left side. Thirty went in—which meant I still had twenty more to make at some point today to reach my goal.

After a water break, I dribbled up and down the driveway left-handed, switching to left-and-right, then left-handed again. I was supposed to do this an hour a day, according to the plan Fitz spelled out for me.

I went back to the layups, missing every one of them. Disgusted, I tossed three-pointers to prove I still had it. After making four in a row, I overshot the fifth one by about ten feet. The ball rolled all the way to the house, right under the bay window.

Inside, Aunt Betty sat with her head bowed and her hand over her eyes.

Oh cripes, I thought. I'm moaning about not getting the star treatment I'm used to, and my aunt is stuck in a wheelchair.

I tossed my ball aside and went back inside. "What's up, Aunt Betty?"

"Nothing."

I plopped on the floor and waited her out.

"Don't you have homework to do, Savannah?"

"It's still summer," I said.

"I meant basketball homework. Your mother said your coach gives you a sheet after every practice."

"Done." I picked at the carpet. Moldy thing was a goat's-vomit green. Probably older than my father. "So what's up, Aunt Betty?"

"I'm thinking about selling the sheep," she finally said.

"What! Why?"

She glared at me. "Do I look like I'm in any shape to take care of them?"

"You look—"

"Don't you dare say I look good. That's what they say about corpses. *She looks so good.*"

"You look pretty much like crap, Aunt Betty."

"Thank you. Someone willing to speak the truth."

"But why sell the sheep? I thought they didn't really need much care. They eat grass and drink water. You got plenty of both."

"How many lambs did we lose this past month, Savannah?"

I hung my head, grunted the answer.

"If you keep livestock," Aunt Betty said, "you have the obligation to do right by them. There's repairs to be made, hay to stack, wool to shear. A new dog to train. A body needs two good legs to get all that done."

The *one thing* Aunt Betty feared—losing the strength to work her farm—had come down on her.

"Is there something I can do to help you, Aunt Betty?"

"You already did. Your father told me you herd the sheep into the barn every night. You didn't have to do that."

Cleaning up sheep poop in the barn every morning was a disgusting task. But there was something about those big eyes and the way lambs hopped in the field that made it impossible for me not to try to keep things okay for them.

"It wasn't so hard once I got the big ones moving in the right direction," I said. "And I wore your rubber boots. Hope that was okay."

"Of course. I understand you took care of Sultana's body for me. That took guts."

I shrugged. Some things are best left buried. Since that night, I'd scooped the remains of three lambs and buried them too. It hadn't seemed right to just leave their scraps at the edge of the woods, where the coyotes had feasted.

After an endless minute, Aunt Betty spoke again. "They thought I was going to die, you know."

"That sucks big-time. I'm sorry."

She straightened in the wheelchair. "I am not planning to do any such thing, at least not anytime soon."

"Sweet."

"Your father is a good man. But he's no use to me with that back of his, made of glass. To keep the farm going, I need someone strong to help."

I got up, leaned on the windowsill so we'd be eye to eye. In some bizarre way, Aunt Betty had just issued the same challenge Fitz had. "I can be strong."

We stared at each other in a weird game of chicken. My aunt willed me to go back outside, and I willed her to smile.

I won.

O⹀O⹀O⹀O⹀

A couple hours later, an old man with a trucker's hat and a tangled beard came to the front door. He had a cute puppy with him.

"I'm George Otis," he said. "Betty's friend from the farm over. You Mark's little girl?"

"Yeah." If you could call six two *little*.

"Pleased to meet you." He stuck his hand out and I shook it, realizing too late he only had a thumb and two fingers. Good thing I was the one who answered the door—Callie would have fainted dead away.

"Come in," I said.

"Can't. Not with the dog."

"Aunt Betty won't mind."

"Nope. Can't give the puppy even a whiff of home cookin'. He'll be sniffing around the house all day and not minding the sheep. Is Betty around?"

"Sure. I'll get her. You want some lemonade or something while you wait?"

He shook his head. "I'll walk Manny here around the yard a bit. But first . . ."

"Yeah?"

"Just so you know, Betty and me been friends a long time. She wouldn't let me see her at the hospital. You tell her, young lady, that I'm refusing to leave the dog with anyone but her."

Holed up in her bedroom, Aunt Betty had a few choice words for Mr. Otis.

"So I'm guessing that means *no*?" I said.

She shrugged, the bones in her shoulders poking up through her blouse.

"What should I tell him?" I said.

"Tell him I'm busy right now. That I'll call him later tonight."

"Okay, but he's going to want to know what you're busy doing. You want me to lie for you, Aunt Betty?"

She sighed. "Of course not. Tell him the truth—that I'm just not myself right now."

"Oh for Pete's sake. Like this guy with a troll beard and three fingers is going to care that you're a little beat up after being in the hospital?"

She straightened in the wheelchair. "Are you insulting my friend, Savannah?"

"You're insulting him by not seeing him. What's up with that?" I took a deep breath, thinking the next shot would be like lobbing a desperation ball from mid-court. "Which is it, Aunt Betty? Are you too stuck-up to be seen not looking your best? Or are you chicken?"

Her eyes narrowed with that teacher's glare that meant you were about to get a lifetime of detention. "Tell George Otis I will be out shortly."

O⹀O⹀O⹀O⹀

Ten minutes later, Aunt Betty had cut the leg of her overalls and somehow got them over that big cast. In her sunhat and white T-shirt, she looked more like herself. I held the door while she wheeled herself out to the front porch. She and Mr. Otis had shared the briefest of greetings—*how ya doing, fine thank you*—and we got down to dog business.

An Anatolian shepherd, Manny had the floppy ears and square jaw of a Labrador retriever but much longer legs. Mr. Otis said he'd weigh as much as me when he was full-grown.

Manny jumped up on me and smothered me with kisses. I snuggled into his fur. He smelled puppy sweet.

"None of that, young lady," Mr. Otis said. "You gotta be strong about this."

"I'm just giving him a hug. That's all."

Aunt Betty shook her head. "Remember what I told you. What you agreed to."

Instead of being my pal, Manny would have to be my job. The pasture would be his hangout and the coyotes, fishers, and foxes his enemies. We couldn't play with him, cuddle him, or let him in the house. He had to live with the sheep until he so identified with them that he'd defend them with his life.

When I said I could be strong, I meant my arms and legs—not my heart. I suddenly missed New Mexico, where I could always get a hug from my teammates, and had friends I could bounce around like a puppy with. Callie had turned into a gym rat, Mom struggled to make it in her new job, Dad studied all the time. It would be nice to have someone to talk to besides Gonzo, even if it was just a dog.

"I have some money saved up," I said. "Maybe I could buy Manny for a pet, and we could get another dog to watch the sheep."

Mr. Otis took off his cap and scratched his wispy gray hair. "You said she was a determined girl, Betty. Not like you to be wrong."

"I'm not," Aunt Betty said. "Am I, Savannah?"

My heart ached as I untangled from Manny. "I know what I have to do. And I will do it."

Mr. Otis nodded. "Good enough. He's all yours."

"Take him out to the kennel, please," Aunt Betty said.

"But he'll be all by himself out there. That's not even near the pasture."

"Pick out a lamb just about his size and put it in with him. And no petting or hugging him."

"And no sweet-talking," Mr. Otis added.

I walked Manny out to the kennel behind the barn. I got some clean straw for bedding, put out some food, and tried to ignore his puppy-dog eyes. "I'm going to get you a lamb to play with," I said as I latched him in. "So you won't be alone."

His eyes sought me out through the chain-link fence. Poor little guy had been taken from the only home he'd ever known, not sure what anyone wanted of him, who his friends would be.

In some really weird, freakish way he reminded me of Callie. And maybe myself too.

CHAPTER TWELVE

The Chester High gym rang with sweet sounds.

Balls rattled the boards. Sneakers squeaked on the floor. Girls dribbled about, a *thum thum* that kept time with my heart.

The Summer Jamboree was a warm-up for the fall tournament season. Fire belonged to the Select Basketball Association, a fall-ball organization that sharpened girls for their upcoming school seasons. Today was my last chance before the season to prove I had boosted my game and to persuade Fitz that I should be the starting center for the team.

In Thursday's practice he had tossed me a pinny. Gonzo high-fived me. Big deal. Lori missed practice because she needed a root canal.

No pinnies today. We were all in our flashy red shirts, with *Fire* scrawled across the front in flame yellow. When the lady in the red glasses passed them out, Gonzo snickered. Clearly Red Glasses had deliberately dyed her hair the same shade as our team colors.

When I saw that woman with Lori, I realized they were mother and daughter. Thankfully, Lori's hair was still the usual light brown.

Fire was slotted in Bracket B, scheduled to play ten-minute games against three other teams. The teams who finished first in the two brackets would play a regulation game after supper. All for fun, the organizers said. No trophies, everyone a winner, *blah blah blah.*

Tell that to a hundred girls just itching to compete.

The starters were the pinny group—Molly, Bailey, Gonzo, Bubble, and Lori. Gonzo gave me a sympathetic shrug as I headed for the bench.

We won the first game by ten points. Gonzo buzzed around the floor like a gnat. I scored six points, had two assists, and three rebounds in the three minutes I played.

We won our second game by four points. To show Molly I wasn't a gunner, I passed off to her every time I got the ball.

"Just shoot the freakin' thing already," she finally yelled.

Mid-afternoon, we fought hard to win our third game, everyone in and out to keep our legs fresh. Going undefeated assured that we'd be playing in the regulation game that *wasn't* a championship.

Gonzo, Olivia, and I sat in the hall, waiting for Bailey to return from the other gym and tell us who we'd be playing.

Olivia pulled a couple of cans of Blue Boost out of her cooler. "Want one?"

Gonzo grabbed one. "Dude, yeah. Pass it here."

"Like you need to buzz," I said. "You're already worse than a hyper two-year-old."

"What about you, Savvy?" Olivia pressed a cold one to my neck, made me jump.

"I never drink the stuff. Too expensive," I said. At the cheapest, Blue Boost ran two bucks a can. It was supposed to give you a ton of energy, but my father said it would rot your stomach. This from the guy who made chili so hot, flames came out my eyeballs.

"Not if you buy it by the case," Olivia said. "That's what my brother does."

"Why?"

"He needs something to keep his energy up. He plays Babe Ruth and Legion baseball. Plus he works almost full-time."

Gonzo downed hers in a single gulp and blessed us with a mighty burp. "Guys on the Red Sox drink this stuff. It's the nectar of champions."

Bailey came around the corner with a glum look and a single word: "Kronos."

"What's Kronos?" I said.

"Not what. That's whose team we're playing." Bailey grabbed a Blue Boost and then slid behind Olivia so she could braid her hair.

"So who is Kronos?"

"The coach of Newport Power—the snottiest, dirtiest, pissyest team in the association. Fitz will want to beat them into the floor. But it won't be easy."

"It never is. Kronos is a beast." Olivia pointed down the hall. "Hey, there's the spawn of Satan now."

Gonzo and I burst out laughing. I expected a biker chick with tats and facial hair, but Kronos looked like she had just stepped out of *Allure* magazine. Her auburn hair hung loose around her shoulders. She had the straight nose and high cheekbones that Alyssa and Callie ooh-ed about in the fashion magazines. The mesh shorts that made the rest of us look like dorks were high style on her, showing off long, tanned legs.

I want to be Kronos when I grow up, I decided.

"Why does Fitz hate her?" Gonzo said.

"She played for him way back when he was still coaching high school," Bailey said. "Word was she was a real big star, probably still holds some Rhode Island scoring records."

Olivia motioned us close, spoke in a ghost-story voice. "Something went really bad her senior year. Nobody knows quite what. And no one's gonna ask Fitz."

"Ooh, spooky," I said. "I'm shakin' in my sneakers."

"Don't make light of what you don't understand, rookie."

Bailey smacked Olivia. "Shut up. Let the young'ns find out for themselves. And you, Savvy Christopher—you will find out. Trust me."

O≈O≈O≈O≈

My parents sat in their usual spot, midway up the bleachers on Fire's offensive side of the court. They'd be better off behind the bench, I thought, for all the playing time I would get tonight.

Fitz sent out our regular starting lineup to begin the game. Gonzo and Bubble were guards, Molly and Bailey were forwards. Lori was in at center. She knew the technical aspects of the game but because she shied away from contact, Lori gave away real estate to pesky forwards on defense and couldn't penetrate to the low post on offense.

I could play the position so much better, if only Fitz would set me loose. Not that he hadn't warned me that this would happen. The 16s would be holding their jamboree here tomorrow. Had I joined that team instead of the Fire, my butt would be in the game, not on the bench.

"The girl dug her hole in the wrong field," Mr. Otis might say if he knew my predicament.

"The girl knew what she was getting into before she picked up the shovel," Aunt Betty would answer.

The horn blew and the game started. I got my head into it, trying to learn what I could, anticipate how I could help my team once I did get onto the court.

For the first few minutes, Fire played the Newport Power close. Ava subbed in, followed by Olivia and some others. I got one minute of play, fouled some skinny girl with a big mouth, and got pulled out of the game before I could even get a shot off. Kronos's team had a five-point lead by the end of the first half.

During the break, a girl with bleached hair came into the gym. Judging from her dirty knees and the monogrammed bat on her jacket, she had just played in a softball tournament. The calendar means nothing to elite athletes who often go from one sport to the other on the same day. You play ice hockey all summer, softball in the fall, basketball any time you can get a gym.

Being the best means you start young and never stop. Sure, a couple of my friends back in New Mexico burned out by the time they were twelve. But I would play basketball 24/7 if my parents would let me.

The new player exchanged cleats for sneakers and slipped on a pair of goggles. "Man, look at how tall she is," Bubble said. "They got a Savvy on their team too."

"Except she looks like she ate Savvy for lunch," Olivia said.

Goggles had to outweigh me by fifty pounds. In the paint,

she'd be like the girl version of Shaq. Lori wouldn't even try to get by her to the basket.

Fitz glanced over at me, rubbed his chin, said nothing. The horn blew and I began the second half on the bench. The score was 20–15, Power in the lead.

Lori scrambled but Goggles scored three baskets in the first two minutes. By the time Fitz finally subbed me in, the period was half over and the score was 30–20.

Goggles took one look at me and grinned like a hungry hyena.

Didn't matter that this was only a jamboree or that Power had a ten-point lead, Coach Kronos had no intention of letting up. Her team went into a full-court press as we inbounded the ball.

Gonzo went up for a shot and got stuffed by a girl with a knife tattoo on her forearm. Bubble stole the ball back. Goggles looked for me on the high post. I deked to the baseline circle, where Bubble found me. *Swish!* 30–23.

They tried to fast-break with a monster pass. Waiting at half-court, I stretched high and knocked the pass to Molly. She and Gonzo went two on one on a Power forward. Gonzo hit from the block.

Less than three minutes left, but we had cut their lead in half.

I glanced at the bench. Lori inched near the scorer's table, itching to come back in. When play started back up after the basket, I was still in the game.

I planted in the lane on defense. Power slowed play by passing around. Finally, their guard bricked a shot. I came down with the ball and sharp elbows, and heard someone go *oomph*. The whistle blew. I looked around to see who I had clobbered.

Gonzo pressed her hand to her face, blood oozing out through her fingers.

"Oh man," I said. "I'm so sorry."

She smiled, showing bloody teeth and braces. "No problem, dude."

During the injury time-out, Coach Kronos came down to our bench. "Are you okay?" Her voice was surprisingly light, like a little kid's.

Fitz shooed her away like she was a mangy cat. Kronos winked at me and went back to her bench. Weird, I thought.

"Fire," the ref called. "Let's go."

Gonzo had to stay out until the bleeding stopped. "Penske, back in at center," Fitz said.

My heart sunk until I heard: "Muir, you switch to guard. Christopher, you move to forward."

"Yes sir."

"All of you—feed Christopher like she ain't eaten in a week."

I nibbled my bottom lip to keep from grinning.

We circled for a *one-two-three Fire!* then broke. As we headed back onto the court, Fitz tapped my shoulder. "Savvy. Hold up."

Savvy? Rumor was he even called his own wife Fitzgerald.

"I know this is just jamboree and all. But"—he gave me a wicked grin—"shoot the lights out."

I had waited six weeks to hear him sing that song.

Five points down, a little over two minutes left. The scoring went back and forth for the first minute. I hit a hook, Power hit on the fast-break. I hit again on a layup, Power hit again. Fire couldn't seem to whittle down those five points.

With a minute left, Molly fed the back to Bubble. I yelled "Pasta" and prayed Lori would set a pick at the top of the key. She did and Goggles pushed around her, expecting me to head for the paint.

Instead, I cut to the far left. Bubble dished me the ball. *Swish!* My three-pointer cut their lead to two points.

Power passed around the perimeter to eat up the clock. I hooked a foot in front of Goggles so she couldn't screen for her guard. She kicked forward and elbowed backward, taking me down. The whistle blew.

As Goggles helped me up, she whispered, "Next time you get in my way—I'll break your face."

"Oh," I said. "Is that what happened to you?"

I went to the free throw line with seven seconds left on the game clock. Sink both and we tie the game. This was just a jamboree. No overtime, not when you're just playing for fun. Coach Fitzgerald had his own reasons for wanting to win this game, but I didn't care whether the opposing coach was Kronos or Justin Timberlake.

Winning was winning.

I bounced the ball, let calm wash over me. The Fire parents cheered me on, the Power side chanted, "Dee-fense."

I willed it all away. The whole world was me, the ball, and that basket.

I bent my knees, rose up, flicked my wrist, and *swish!* Power

30, Fire 29. The ref bounced the ball back to me. Gonzo subbed in, bloody gauze stuffed in both her nostrils.

An idea seized me, something immature and risky. Stupid, really, but maybe not when you practiced it over and over for six weeks like Gonzo and I had. A little kids' play—something no one would expect because an elite team doesn't pull such playground crap.

Then again—winning was winning.

"Hey, Gonzo. Wanna come over later for tacos?" I said.

She raised her eyebrows, glanced at the bench. "Um . . . okay, sure. What time?"

"Seven," I said, indicating the spot on the rim of the basket that corresponded with a clock.

"Let's go, Fire," the ref barked out.

"Sure you don't want to stick with the regular menu?" Gonzo said.

"No. Tacos." I acted the part, showing no muscle and all finesse. At the very last moment, I whipped the ball, clunking it hard off the rim. Before anyone had a chance to react, I leaped forward and grabbed my own rebound.

Goggles got on me, arms raised to block the shot. That wasn't the play anyway. To my right, Lori waved at me, begging for the ball.

I looked left, found Gonzo exactly where she was supposed to be—sneaking along the baseline. She stepped right, drawing her guard up the lane. Then she reversed, sinking a pretty layup from the left side.

The horn blew, ending the game.

Fire 31, Power 30.

CHAPTER THIRTEEN

The girls jumped all over Gonzo, celebrating like this was the national championship and not some meaningless jamboree game.

I was about to join the crowd when Lori got in my face. "I was open," she said. "You saw me. I know you saw me."

"It all happened so fast—"

"I had the shot, Savvy. I had the shot but you looked me off."

"Sorry."

She narrowed her eyes. "No, you're not."

"For Pete's sake, Lori. Everything was going light speed. I made a mistake."

"You saw me, decided *no, she can't do it*. So you go looking for your binkie. Gonzo's in traffic but so what? Savvy Christopher and her little pet can do anything. Why even bother playing five on the court when Gonzalez and Christopher are out there?"

I lowered my voice. "Sheesh, Lori. Let it go, will you? I said I was sorry."

She straightened her shoulders. "You don't get it, do you?"

"Get what?"

"You have no respect for the blessing you've been given."

"We talking religion now?"

Lori stomped away, muttering over her shoulder. "Just freakin' forget it."

"I already did," I yelled, but Lori's outburst dug under my skin like a splinter. So what if Gonzo was my security blanket? Everyone needed someone who would always be where you could find them. Someone you could trust to do what you needed doing. Someone you knew could make the shot.

Next time I'd take the stupid shot myself.

⊙-⊙-⊙-⊙-

I had a near heart attack when I saw my parents chatting with Coach Kronos in the parking lot.

Kronos smiled, shook my hand. "We haven't been officially introduced. I'm Jennifer Kronos."

"Savvy. Savvy Christopher." My tongue stuck to the roof of my mouth. If Fitz saw us, he'd go ballistic.

Mom beamed with excitement. "Jennifer recognized your father and wanted to say hello."

"When I first got married," Kronos said, "I'd spend Saturdays and Sundays watching golf with my husband. I saw your dad win a couple of the majors."

"That was a long time ago," Dad said. "Injuries and all."

Kronos nodded sympathetically. "I didn't even make it through college ball. Tore my knee apart in the Sweet Sixteen."

"You played in the Sweet Sixteen?" I said.

"Yeah. For Pat Summit."

"You went to Tennessee?" For as long as I could remember, I had dreamed about wearing orange for the Lady Vols.

"Pat's a great coach. Phenomenal."

We stood in silence for a moment, giving Pat Summit the respect she deserves.

"I was telling Jennifer about the move," my mother said.

"A change is always tough," Kronos said. "How's your new team working out for you?"

"Um. Good."

"Savvy's been quite happy with the Fire," Dad said.

"That's great. Of course." Kronos flashed him a quick smile but saved the full wattage for me. "I can see you're headed for a great career, Savvy. You may have noticed that I've got a couple players with a future."

Goggles had a great future, all right. Smackin' down for the WWE.

"Good for us that your coach rested you for the first half," she said. "Or you might have really clobbered us."

Ouch.

"Like I said, Fire is a great team—"

She didn't say that, I thought.

"—but I'm not sure they're in a position to go national. Especially if you, Savvy, don't get to start. I really need a power forward. You'd fit that role perfectly."

I wiped my sweaty palms on my shorts. "I play center."

Kronos locked her eyes on mine. "You're wasted at center, and wasted even worse on the bench. That wouldn't happen on my team."

Mom pasted on her work smile, the kind that said the customer was always right. Dad scratched his eyebrow, said nothing. Kronos was recruiting me away from Fire and they apparently were leaving the decision to me.

"My friends play for Fire," I said.

"Sure, I understand. You'll have plenty of time to worry about higher goals."

The only way my goal could be higher was if I expected to play for the NBA with Tim Duncan, instead of the WNBA with Diana Taurasi.

I wanted national now. I wanted to play for Kronos like *yesterday*. But if I said I would do something, I did it—whether it's cleaning up after sheep or cleaning up after Lori. And if I switched teams, I'd lose the only real friend I had.

"I guess I'm okay for now," I said.

Kronos held out a business card. "Let me give you my number, in case you ever want to chat. Get the inside scoop on what Tennessee looks for in a recruit."

Mom snatched the card. "I'll grab this so it won't get lost. Savvy hasn't cleaned out that bag of hers since the stone ages."

We waved good-bye and piled into the car. Mom passed me a ham sandwich and chatted on about the game. I fed my face and considered my options.

I could still switch teams. The rosters wouldn't be set until a few days before the first official tournament, the weekend after Labor Day.

Leaving Gonzo would suck. Getting off the bench and starting for a top team would be awesome. Playing forward instead of center would make better use of my shooting.

Playing with that gorilla Goggles would make me puke. Playing for a coach who had been coached by Pat Summit would be the next-best thing to playing for the great one herself.

If there was one thing I'd be tempted to sell my soul for, it was basketball.

Maybe I would call Kronos in a couple of days, see what she thought about wearing a mitten on the dominant hand during practice. She'd probably think it was child abuse—although, judging by the dirty tactics of her team, maybe they practiced with tacks in their sneakers.

As I enjoyed the notion of Goggles with bloody feet, my cell buzzed. Ava? Whoa. She'd never called me before.

"Hey," I said. "What's up?"

"I saw you talking to Kronos."

"Yeah, she kind of knows my father. Well, not really knows him—"

"Of course not," Ava said, cutting me off. "She saw you wipe that stupid team of hers like the rags they are and she wants you. Don't do it. All right?"

"Um . . . okay."

"Fine. I'm calling you tomorrow, just in case you forget your promise."

"Yeah, but—"

"Later."

I clicked off, only to get a *bing*. A text message had come in from Molly. Someone else who never had a good word for me but now told me *d/g*—don't go.

I texted back *y?*

She rang me up. "Purely selfish reasons. I like playing with you because teams have to double you. That frees me up to score."

"Yeah. Sure."

Molly snorted. "These coaches are like vultures. After that performance, you'll get calls from eastern Connecticut to southern Massachusetts. When you do, remember you're very young to be playing with the eighteens."

"I know," I said, tempted to add that she'd been reminding me of that for six weeks.

"You need us to watch out for you. Plus you and Gonzo will be on the high school team next year with me and Bailey. It's not too early to be talking about next year's state championship. Ava's talking about transferring from the vocational school, so that would make five of us. Don't screw up our chemistry—"

We have chemistry? I thought.

"—by doing something stupid."

"I won't."

"Excellent. Can I come see your dog sometime?"

"Huh? You want to see my dog?"

"I love dogs. Didn't you know?"

"Um . . . no." Because you don't talk to me, you idiot. "Sure, you can come anytime. But we can't play with Manny."

"I know that. I've already done the research on livestock dogs. I've wanted to see an Anatolian shepherd for some time. Let's do it soon."

"Sure, soon." I closed the phone, my head spinning. I had gone from being an eighth-grade cancer to someone the team couldn't live without.

Thank you, Fitz. And thank you, Kronos.

CHAPTER FOURTEEN

A couple days later Gonzo and I were sitting on the front porch when Alyssa came by to take Callie to the mall. She smiled, patted me on the head, and went inside the house to move Callie along. The car was stuffed with cheerleaders. They gave Gonzo and me a quick look, then went on with their chatter.

Alyssa and Callie came out five minutes later and caught us arguing.

"You got to choose last time," I said. "It's my turn to pick the movie."

"You have sucky taste," Gonzo said. "And you always like my choices, once we get there."

Callie breezed on by us without another look. She wore white short-shorts and an orange tank top that showed a lot of skin. Alyssa wore the same outfit, except her top was royal blue. If we rolled the other cheerleaders out of the car, they'd probably be in the same outfit and look just as pukey cute.

Alyssa squeezed between us on the front porch and sat down. "What's up, ladies?"

"Savvy wants to go see *Summer Rose,*" Gonzo said.

"Ooh, Savvy. I never took you for a romantic," Alyssa said.

I blushed. My choice was a teen romance in which the hot kid like Marc falls in love with the artistic girl. Someday

Hollywood would get it right and the girl would be a jock in sweats instead of a creative type in overalls and glasses.

"I want to see *Dog Days*," Gonzo said.

"Never heard of it," Alyssa said.

I reached around her to slap Gonzo. "Because it stinks."

"No, the critics say it's"—Gonzo put on a cheap British accent—"'rib-cracking hilarious. Social satire at its sharpest.'"

"A waste of seven bucks," I said.

Gonzo turned to Alyssa to plead her case. "See, this sorority is getting sued because they discriminate against ugly girls. So they hold a pledge drive and recruit all these dogs—"

"Real dogs?" Alyssa said.

"No, dude. Woofer girls. Anyway, they think girls this nasty will prove to the judge they don't discriminate. And of course, two of the pledges turn out to be goofy guys dressed as girls, and all the usual garbage ensues. The head cheerleader—no offense—falls for one of the guys. But in the end, he goes for one of the ugly girls. Who isn't ugly once she puts on a little lipstick and takes off her glasses."

"Talk about a cliché," I said.

Alyssa stood, glared down on us. "No kidding. A girl takes the time and energy to be nice to everyone, to look terrific, and suddenly, she's a bitch."

Callie yelled from the backseat, "Hey, the girls want to get going."

Alyssa gave us a dirty look, got in the car, and drove off.

"Man, your sister really clicked into that clique." Gonzo poked me. "Get it? The pun, I mean."

"I think Alyssa just feels sorry for my sister."

"You kidding, dude?" Gonzo picked a scab on her knee. "Your sister is one of them, a perfect clone down to the sparkly sandals and the shiny lip gloss."

"That's because she's a . . . what do you call those lizards? They blend into the surroundings."

"Chameleons?"

"The popular kids always like her because she looks good and doesn't say enough to piss anyone off."

"Except you," Gonzo said.

"Yeah. Piss me off and what does she lose? Nothing."

"*Dog Days,*" Gonzo said. "I'm telling you, we gotta go to the dogs. I read that people in the audience bark at the sorority princesses. Won't that feel good?"

What would feel good would be to live in the world of *Summer Rose,* where the incredible guy falls for the girl who could shoot the lights out.

Someday I'd make my own movie, and get it right.

O=O=O=O=

We went upstairs so I could put on sneakers to bike to the movies.

Stupid Callie hadn't done the laundry, so I dug under the bunk bed, looking for an old pair of socks.

"You got plenty in your gym bag," Gonzo said.

"Hey. You know better," I said. "Don't even go there."

"Right. The lucky socks that no one can approach unless they're wearing a Haz-Mat suit."

"Luck doesn't come free. It takes dedication and commitment."

I pushed out from under the bed, brushed dust off my shirt, and tried not to think of my old room in New Mexico with my double bed, walk-in closet, and my own bathroom. *That* room I kept clean.

"Yo, Savannah. Ever occur to you that lucky socks are juvie?"

"Yo, Nina. Tradition is tradition. I wear one pair of socks all weekend for a tournament. If we win, I enshrine them."

"You ought to embalm them."

"Grief, you sound like Lori." I wiggled my arm between the wall and my mattress. "I dumped some laundry on my bed. Maybe it slipped down behind here."

"Your shoulders are too big. Move it. I'll look." Gonzo squeezed under the bed and disappeared behind the boxes we hadn't unpacked.

We told Mom it was because we had no place to put our stuff. Deep down, both Callie and I prayed that some miracle—maybe winning the lottery—would allow us to go back to New Mexico.

If we did that, I'd want to keep sheep. But I'd be sure to get the biggest, meanest guardian dog ever. I was daydreaming about fluffy white sheep against the high mountains and bright blue sky when Gonzo yelped from under the bed.

"Look what I found." She wriggled out, a scale in her hand.

"Must be Callie's," I said.

"Nice. Expensive."

"She's good for it. All that babysitting back in New Mexico."

"It's one of those programmable ones. It stores your weight so you can see if you're gaining or losing." Gonzo gave me a wicked smile. "Let's see how much she weighed before the whole going-to-the-gym-with-Alyssa thing started."

"She'll freak if she finds out."

"Come on. You think she wouldn't snoop on you?"

"Yeah, okay. Just don't screw it up so she can find out."

Gonzo tapped the buttons. Numbers scrolled on the little screen. "The first number is one twenty-five. Cripes, I weigh one fifteen. What's wrong with that?"

"It's heavy for a flier. The base has to be able to boost them so they can do those aerial stunts."

"When did she get reamed out by the coach?"

"Almost a month ago. But that's all in the past—she got back onto the active squad a couple weeks ago."

"This ain't good, dude. Look. Seventeen pounds. My mother does Weight Watchers," Gonzo said. "She talks ten pounds max in a month."

"Go down a little more," I said. "See? She's gained back six. So maybe a bunch of it was water weight. That can come off real fast. And she has put on some muscle, going to the gym every day."

"This yo-yo stuff goes against all those lectures we get in health class," Gonzo said. "Maybe you should tell your mother or someone."

"Oh no. And you're keeping your mouth shut on this."

She shrugged. "Yeah, okay. I got my own sisters to rag on."

After I got back from seeing the stinky *Dog Days,* the discovery ate at me for the rest of the afternoon. That dumb attempt to vomit into the wastebasket seemed to be a one-time only. With Alyssa pushing her, Callie had worked her tail off, three hours a day at the gym. Maybe the flab had melted so fast because it wasn't meant to be there in the first place.

I was in the middle of making salad for supper when Mom got home from work. She made a few minutes of chitchat before asking: "Has Callie said anything about how cheering is going?"

"Not really."

"She won't say, of course. But she is looking good these days."

"Uh-huh." I chopped the carrots double-time.

"You don't think she's a little too thin, do you?"

Kick a hole in the dam, why don't you? Once I started spilling, I couldn't stop.

CHAPTER FIFTEEN

Callie came in from cheerleading and caught us looking at her scale. "What is going on here?"

"Your sister wanted me to see this," Mom said. "She's concerned about your weight loss."

"My sister should mind her own business."

"I'm concerned too. Girls your age are under tremendous pressure to adjust their bodies to fit society's norms."

"Oh please, I'm not some dumb girl in some dumb Lifetime movie."

I edged toward the door. As interesting as it was that Callie had exploded instead of imploding, Mom didn't need my help fanning the flames. Dad had come home and must have heard the yelling. He stood in the hall, trying to make sense of this.

Mom blabbed on. "Girls are driven to try things that aren't healthy. Diet pills, laxatives, fasts, purging. A weight loss this rapid can't be good. Honey, are you bulimic?"

"This is so stupid," Callie said. "Savvy, tell her that I am not puking up meals."

"How would she know?" Dad said, finally clued in.

"Yeah. How would I know?" I said.

"You're the toilet police. Sniffing after every meal."

"Is this true, Savvy?" Dad said.

I nodded.

"Why would you do that?"

Callie dug her fingernails into my arm. "Never mind. It's nothing."

I yanked away. "I found her about a month ago, trying to make herself throw up."

"I was sick to my stomach, didn't think I'd make it to the bathroom. You had no freakin' right to make a big deal out of this, Savvy."

"Hold it," Dad said. "She has every right. She's your sister. She cares about you."

"Did it ever. Occur. To anybody"—the veins in Callie's neck popped—"that you smother me with all this so-called caring?"

"You've got to be kidding," I muttered under my breath.

Mom passed the scale to my father. "Mark, look at this. According to Savvy, this weight loss was prompted by her getting benched in cheerleading on the first day."

"You told them that too? Savvy, you swore on your heart you wouldn't."

I wanted out of this mess, but Dad blocked the door. "All this weight in less than a month," he said. "This is a concern."

Callie ripped the scale away. "So I lost some weight, so what? I can't believe the stupid big deal you're making out of this."

"Why don't we all calm down," Mom said.

"A girl tries to tone up, get in good shape, and suddenly it's a made-for-TV movie. And you"—Callie turned her scalding gaze my way—"you freak of nature—"

"Callie, don't get personal, please," Dad said.

"—you had no right to snoop through my things."

"I just tried to help." Sheesh. Take the best shot and catch crap for it.

"I get you're the big star around here. Fine, live long and prosper with your moronic basketball. But it's not fair that I have you in my face every second. I've got no privacy, no space, nothing but you smelling like sweat and dog and sheep crap. When the flippin' hell are you gonna grow up, Savvy? I can't bear to bring my friends here because you're al—"

"Me? You're the one this freakin' family revolves around. Everything's about making sure you're not scared or upset, making sure you're talking, making sure—"

"I don't need anyone to do anything but leave me alone!"

"Stop it," Mom said. "Stop it now."

"No, you stop it," I said. "Stop babying her and make her grow up."

"You're the baby. Gotta be fed every two hours or you cry," Callie said.

"Enough," Dad said. "I'd like you to get on the scale, Callie."

"No. No friggin' way." Her voice was husky.

"Yes."

My sister curled her lips into her teeth, trying to hide her smile. "You go ahead and make me, Dad."

"Oh, that's just evil," I said.

"What's evil is this cross-examination. All you have to do is look at me to see I'm fine. Just look."

Callie tossed her bag onto the top bunk, then stretched her

arms out. She was a little puffy in the face, but in shorts and a tank top, it was clear that she'd regained the wiry muscles that made her such a great tumbler.

"What's this?" Mom said. A couple of pill bottles had plopped out of my sister's bag.

"Just some vitamins. All-natural. Give me those."

Mom passed them to my father. "Where did you get these?" he said.

"The health food store. They're herbal stuff. Legal and safe."

Dad frowned as he studied the ingredients. "From what I understand, hoodia is a scam. Products containing ephedrine are downright dangerous."

"They wouldn't sell them if they were dangerous."

"They don't care," Dad said. "They just want the money. We're flushing these. And don't you buy any more, young lady."

"Are these all the pills you have?" my mother said.

If my sister's stare were any more poisonous, we'd be dead on the floor. "Yes. Go ahead, search my bag if you don't believe me."

Dad grabbed her bag, came up with lip gloss, a ten-dollar bill, and breath mints. "No more of this," he said. "Do you understand me, Callie?"

"Why are you doing this to me? I try to get healthy and you jump on me like I'm some druggie or anorexic or something."

My mother smoothed her hair. "It's been a tough move, baby. We only want to make sure you're okay."

Callie pawed at her tears. "Finally we're getting around to admitting that? After all those months of happy-face garbage? Did it ever occur to you that I might not want to come to this stinkin' sheep farm?"

"I'm sorry, honey," Dad said. "I knew the move was hard for you. And it is unfair—I screwed up royally, and you girls and your mother are stuck with the damage."

"Daddy, no. Don't say that," I said.

His eyes blurred up, like he was going to cry now. Why didn't Callie say something? All the energy we put into making her feel better—she should give something back once in a while. But this family was one sick merry-go-round. Callie felt guilty because she thought Dad's accident was her fault, Dad felt guilty because he let the family down, Mom did everything she could to cover up their guilt and pretend everyone was happy.

No wonder I enjoyed the sheep. Things were a lot simpler out under the sky.

Dad put his hands on Callie's shoulders, looked her in the eye. "Mom and I reserve the right to search your belongings if we have any concern at all about your welfare. Do you understand?"

"Nice, Dad. Really nice. What. Ever." Callie hopped up onto the bunk and plugged into her iPod.

Mom and Dad took the supplements and went out of the room, leaving me with the *look* and the scale.

Nice. Really nice.

O≈O≈O≈O≈

Three weeks ago, I had moved the sheep up to the high pasture so the grass in the low one could grow back. Each evening when I pushed Aunt Betty up there in her wheelchair, she'd throw out some interesting fact. She'd point out the red-tailed hawks high overhead, tracking mice in the grass. Tell me that tangy-smelling weed by the fence made a nice tea. Wondered about how many pounds of wool we'd shear this fall.

Aunt Betty had nothing to say this evening. That was fine with me.

When we got up there, she got onto her crutches and hobbled along the fence, checking for termites in the wooden posts, thistles that could sicken livestock, off-color turds that meant a sheep was sick.

Any excuse to keep busy and feel needed.

Week by week, we expanded Manny's territory. After moving him from a small pen with one lamb to a larger one with three lambs, we now allowed him to hang out with the flock. Tonight, I leashed him and walked around the perimeter of the pasture—the first time on the outside of the fencing. Each long circle took us a little closer to the woods.

Something rustled in the brush. The fur on Manny's neck went up. He strained, his nose sniffing. Would a coyote fly out of that tangle of trees, its fangs aimed at my throat? Would Manny protect me, like he tried to protect the sheep? He was big and sturdy but still so young.

It was wrong of us to think he could guard the sheep by himself. But what choice did we have?

"Hey!" I yelled. A fat quail flew out of the brush.

Manny's shoulders tensed, wanting to spring. I made him sit, turned his head back toward the flock. After a minute of obedience, we returned to the pasture, where I unleashed him. He circled the sheep, like he needed to count heads.

Aunt Betty got into her chair and we started for home. She finally spoke. "Don't know if it's a good thing or a bad thing—but when your sister gets going, she has quite the voice."

I didn't know if this was a good thing or bad thing either.

CHAPTER SIXTEEN

Mom stayed home from work the next morning. Something was up.

She'd been pounding all of New England, selling printer supplies and trying to make enough commission so that someday—when our bankruptcy was just a bad aftertaste and Dad had a new career—we'd be able to buy another house.

Alyssa pulled into the driveway around seven thirty to take Callie to the gym.

"Alyssa's here," I said.

Callie glared at me as she pulled on her sports bra. Her ribs had reappeared, along with the start of a six-pack on her abdomen. She had worked herself into incredible shape.

"Wow," I said.

Callie shoved me aside just in time to see Mom chatting up Alyssa. "Oh no, she's gonna ask her about the pills. Savvy, get down there and stop her. Hurry up!"

I ran down the stairs, irked that my sister was suddenly talking to me again, now that she needed something.

Alyssa greeted me with a smile and a wave. "Hey, Sav. I stopped at the Tall-tales in the mall. They're bringing in a shipment of jeans in extra-longs. You wear size four, right?"

"Thanks," I said. "But I wear eight."

Callie yelled from the window, "Mom, I think your cell phone is ringing."

My mother didn't fall for it—her cell was hooked onto the waist of her suit pants.

"Your mom and I were just talking about the barn," Alyssa said.

"The barn?" Okay, so my mother wasn't grilling her. Yet.

Callie came down just in time to hear Mom say, "Wouldn't the barn be a great place to hold a party? Maybe a Labor Day blowout."

"For your customers, right?" Callie said, breathless.

Mom smiled. "No. For your friends."

"What? No . . . you can't . . . I mean, the barn is gross."

"It has vast potential," my mother said.

My sister glanced at me with imploring eyes. Screw her— let her fight her own battles for once.

"We'd be disturbing Aunt Betty," she said.

"I talked to Aunt Betty about it last night."

"Without asking me? How could you?"

"She is all for it."

Callie turned to Alyssa. "Tell her, Alyssa. No one will want to come. People go away for that weekend."

"Not us," Alyssa said. "Football and cheering have practices Saturday and Monday."

"See, Mom? We'd be too busy. Tell her, Alyssa. We'll be exhausted."

Tell her, Alyssa, I thought. Tell her to speak for herself.

"I think it's an astounding idea," Alyssa said.

"Huh?" Callie's eyes popped so wide, she looked like a clown doll.

"It's such a big space, we could invite the whole squad and the football team. Would that be all right, Mrs. Christopher?"

Mom grinned. "Sure."

I almost fell out of my flip-flops when Callie said, "If you think it'll work, Alyssa . . . sure. I'm in."

"Hey, Savvy," Alyssa said. "The guys will outnumber us more than two to one. Why don't you invite your basketball team too?"

If looks could kill, Callie's drove a sword through my heart.

O≡O≡O≡O≡

When Dad got home from school that night, he was furious. "Terri, you invited almost a hundred teenagers, more than half of whom are young men who are living on six thousand calories a day. Are you out of your mind?"

"Alyssa is going to ask the girls to bring things. Brownies and the like," Mom said.

"Oh, that is just ducky. We'll end up with ten pans of brownies and six bags of potato chips." My father rubbed his face. "Is there some way to just have snacks and not a full-blown picnic?"

"We already told everyone it was a picnic. You are doing everything possible to destroy me!" Callie burst into hot tears, shoved me into the refrigerator, and ran out of the room.

Like, what did I do, other than just be big enough to be in the precious one's way? When did she get so loud? I missed the peaceful days of the lump under the covers, saying nothing.

"I'll speak to George Otis," Aunt Betty said. "I'm sure we'll work something out."

Mr. Otis traded us forty pounds of hamburger and six bushels of corn in exchange for being able to graze his cows in Aunt Betty's northwest pasture. That was a fair trade, but I knew he was soft on Aunt Betty when he did something that went far beyond bartering.

He offered to roast a pig for the party.

"Okay, we can make this happen," Dad said. "I'll make baked beans and a couple huge pans of baked apples."

"The absolute coolest," I heard Alyssa tell Callie. "No one's ever done a pig roast before."

O⊫O⊫O⊫O⊫

The day before the picnic, Callie and I had to dig a hole behind the barn to roast the pig.

"A pig on a spit? I'm gonna die," she said.

"Maybe it'll work out," I said.

"And maybe pigs fly."

"No. In this case, pigs die."

"Oh grief, tell me he's not slaughtering the pig here." Callie glanced at the back patio, where Aunt Betty and Mr. Otis sat in lawn chairs, drinking iced tea and making small talk. "Savvy, go ask him."

I dug deep, shoveled up a huge rock. "Why should I?"

She wiped her face, leaving muddy tracks on her cheeks. "Look, I'm sorry I freaked. Mom just gets too in your face."

"Oh, and you weren't?"

"I'm sorry. Really. And I'm glad you and your friends are coming to the party."

"You are?" It would pay for me to suck up to my sister so I could ask if Marc was coming. "I'll go talk to Mr. Otis about the pig."

I brushed the dirt off my hands and walked over to the back of the house, where my aunt and George Otis were deep in conversation.

"They say it's going to be a raw winter," Aunt Betty was saying.

Mr. Otis nodded. "Yep. Jet stream pushing too much moisture in from the water. You hear old Jonas Welker's been dosing his cows?"

"A damn shame." Aunt Betty spotted me. "You need something, Savannah?"

"What are you talking about, dosing cows? Like, Pepto-Bismol or something?" Could sheep catch an illness from cows? Mr. Otis would be moving his cows into the next pasture and—

Whoa, I thought. Better be careful or I'd turn into Aunt Betty.

"Antibiotics," Aunt Betty said.

Even worse. "We're not talking mad cow disease, are we?"

She shook her head. "He's not doing it for a specific infection. He just wants to pack on some extra weight."

"Messin' around with nature's design just to coax out a few extra pounds of beef ain't right," Mr. Otis said.

"What can I do for you, Savannah?" Aunt Betty said.

I asked about slaughtering the pig.

"Did you want to help?" Mr. Otis said.

I shivered. "No!"

"I'll be doing it at my place," Mr. Otis said. "So as to not unsettle anyone."

Aunt Betty squeezed his hand before going back to her iced tea and talk about dosing cows.

I passed on the good news to Callie and got back to digging. "Do you think they'll ever like, get together?" I said. "Married or something?"

"Oh, please. Those two getting it on is too gross to even consider," Callie said. "They're ancient. Holy crap, Savvy. Thanks for putting that disgusting image in my head."

"Wait a minute. You think they're different inside from us, just because they're wrinkly on the outside?"

As she jammed her shovel into the dirt, her biceps popped out like lemons. Alyssa had really helped whip her back into shape. "What are you talking about?"

"Okay, check it out. I just keep getting taller and taller—"

She grunted. "Duh."

"—but I feel like I did when I was like, in fourth grade. Like nothing's changed except my shoe size and the length of my pants."

"Isn't that the stupidest thing? You get older and have to go to high school and have parties even though you're no smarter than you were when you were little. But people expect you to act different." Callie's groan sounded rough, like Manny's morning bark.

"What's wrong with your voice? You're not smoking, are you?"

"Gross. It's allergies, that's all."

"What are you allergic to?"

"Look around. Rhode Island is one big weed." She tossed the shovel like a javelin into the dirt pile and took off.

Wonderful. She takes off—just when I was going to ask if Marc Sardakis was coming to the picnic.

SEPTEMBER

CHAPTER SEVENTEEN

The entire cheerleading squad came out the day before the picnic to decorate the barn. Most of them did the standard double take when they saw me.

"Whoa, you look just like your sister," a redhead named Morgan said. "But you're . . . you're . . ."

I flipped out my usual stupid comeback. "Yeah, it's a shame that Callie is such a runt, isn't it?"

A bouncy girl named Natasha ran to greet me like we had been friends forever. "Olivia Jeffries is my best friend. She talks about you all the time."

"She does?"

"Yeah, she says you're really a great player and she enjoys shooting with you after practice."

What Olivia enjoyed was shooting with Marc and whatever jock friends hung around to play HORSE with us.

We worked for hours to get ready for the party. Mom had been right about the barn—cleaned out and decorated, it was beyond cool. Callie was so excited, she vaulted the fence, did a walkover and a backflip, then dismounted with a double somersault.

My mother had a heart attack, but everyone else watched with open mouths.

"Wow, I didn't know she could do that," Gonzo said.

"It's the one thing she's really good at." I felt a pang of

guilt about the whole scale thing. Didn't my sister have the right to do whatever it took to hold on to her *one thing*?

That night Callie tossed and turned, the squeaking springs on her bunk keeping me up. When I went downstairs to sleep in the living room, I noticed a glow from behind the barn. I grabbed a flashlight and ran out to find Mr. Otis sitting by the fire.

"Huh?" I said. "You still here?"

"Someone's got to babysit the pig all night," he said. "Otherwise, coyotes, raccoons, and fishers will find a way to get at it."

"That's really nice of you to do this. Thank you."

"Right enough, young lady. Betty says you're doin' a fine job with Manny, with the training and all."

I scuffed the ground. "We lost another lamb last week."

"Nature," he said. "We just live here."

"So why bother with livestock dogs at all?"

"It's unnatural to put all that meat in one place. We've got to even the odds some."

"Okay . . ." I backed away. "Thanks for the chat."

He gave me a wave with his three fingers, leaned back in his chair, and pushed his cap down over his face.

O≈O≈O≈O≈

The next morning, I practiced my dribbling and left-handed shooting before anyone was even awake. Halfway through the session, I had to pee so bad, my eyeballs turned yellow. I caught Callie in the bathroom, doing something very bizarre.

"Are you plucking a hair off your chin?" I said.

She spat a juicy swear at me, finishing up with: "Just popping a zit, that's all. Get out."

"Some hairy zit you got there."

"Look, every girl has hair on her face. You just don't realize it because we bleach and pluck."

I rubbed my chin, expecting one to sprout any minute.

"This is no different from plucking your eyebrows or shaving your legs," Callie said. "Something a woman has do."

"If you say so."

"But it is not something you talk about. If you tell anyone about this, I swear—I'll tell about when you got your first period. I mean it, Savvy."

I had been away with a friend's family and was too embarrassed to tell her or her mother, so I made due with paper towels for a full week.

"Fine," I said.

What did I care, as long as my face didn't start popping with a George Otis beard.

O⸱-O⸱-O⸱-O⸱-

The cheerleaders arrived early, chattering like chipmunks. The football players filtered in a few at a time. Gonzo and I sat on the stone wall by the driveway, checking out the guys as they passed.

I twirled a basketball with my left hand and pretended I didn't even notice tens of guys pouring onto Aunt Betty's farm—until Marc Sardakis came around the bend. Startled, I dropped the ball and had to chase after it.

Marc and I got to it at the same time. "Hey, Hotshot," he said.

If he would only let go of the ball, maybe I could breathe. Those clear blue eyes under black eyelashes were fatal.

"What're you doing here?" he said. "You're not a cheerleader."

"Um . . . I'm . . . Callie's sister."

He tilted his head, studied me. "Oh yeah, you do look alike. How old are you anyway?"

I blushed. "Fourteen."

"Starting high school Wednesday, huh?"

"No. Eighth grade. Because . . ." I swallowed, trying to find the guts to keep talking.

Marc smiled, patiently waiting.

"The town we came from in New Mexico starts kids late in school. The cutoff was July, so because I have an August birthday, I was always the oldest kid in my grade. My father says it'll be good for basketball because I'll be physically mature."

"Yeah, I'm already sixteen but going into sophomore year. My father had me slated for sports before I started kindergarten, so they held me back a year."

"Oh."

"Well, I guess I'd better go pay my respects to Callie. Catch you for some hoops later?"

Dork of the century, my mouth had gone dry. My lips stuck to my teeth, so the best I could manage was a nod.

"Good lookin' out, ladies." Marc walked away, my eyes glued to his every step. He was tall enough, young enough, nice enough. A real three-pointer.

My heart went *swish*.

When Olivia and Bailey arrived ten minutes later, we took them up to the party.

The barn rocked with music. Tables were piled with goodies. Alyssa brought over a couple of blow-up rafts so people could troll around the pond. Dad hauled out his golf clubs and turned the lower pasture into a driving range.

Callie looked tan and lean in her black tank top, white shorts, and silver sandals. Her hair was pulled back to show big silver hoops. When we came into the barn, she greeted us with a wave and a grin.

Wow. Okay. So I wasn't the most evil sister ever spawned by uncaring parents.

Gonzo grabbed me, trying to whisper over the music. "I'll keep Olivia and Bailey out of your face. Find Marc and make your move."

"What move? I don't have a move."

"You are so lame. Okay, let me translate. I'll set the pick and you roll off it."

"He's not interested in me. He was just being polite."

"Girl, he lasered you up and down."

"He was just shocked not to see me all sweaty."

"You still gotta take the shot."

"In a minute. I want to go out back and see if Mr. Otis took the pig off the fire yet." All morning I had crept around like a caveman, sniffing out the roasting meat and trying not to drool.

Gonzo rolled her eyes but followed me out the back door. The pig was still on the spit, looking so good that I wanted to tear off a chunk with my bare hands. Aunt Betty and Mr. Otis sat side by side, their heads almost touching as they chatted.

"Well, well. Romance is in the air," Gonzo said. "You can't fail, Hotshot."

I smacked her. "Shut up. They can't hear over the music, that's why they're so close."

She nagged me back inside, still on the hunt for Marc. We found him doing the weird handshake and chest bump thing guys do with their teammates.

Catching my eye, he smiled.

Gonzo jammed her elbow into my ribs. I pushed through the crowd, desperately trying to think of things to say to him—even though I'd been practicing for a week.

You a Pats fan? No, too obvious.

LeBron or Kobe? Interesting, but maybe too sporty.

How do you survive being a punching bag for linebackers and safeties? Something I was curious about, but even thinking about his bruised and battered body made me sweat.

What college are you going to go to? Ugh. Something that Mom would ask.

Do you like dogs? Yeah, that was the one. Everyone likes dogs. *Hey Marc, you like dogs? I'm training one now. No, I never even had one—too busy with sports. But my aunt has these sheep and we have these coyotes . . .*

I was almost to him, the words on my tongue, ready to roll off. Not spit out, I reminded myself. Don't rush the shot. Be natural and smooth. Flex and fly.

I was just a few feet away when the fat kid with the spiked

hair grabbed his arm and said, "Callie's dad is this famous golfer. You gotta come outside, see what he set up. And he's giving out pointers."

Before I could even whimper one word, Marc disappeared with his buddies.

Way to spoil the shot, Dad.

CHAPTER EIGHTEEN

The sad truth was this: I wasn't party material. I couldn't work into any crowd like Gonzo and get people laughing, or let a crowd surround me like Callie and let people think I was the sweetest kid in the world.

While Marc and his buddies golfed, I decided to grab my basketball and work on my game. Fitz's voice never left my head for long. *You gotta dribble as well with your left hand as your right, Christopher. Confound your opponents so they don't know where the heck you're coming at them from.*

Okay, I could dribble two balls at once now. The left side was ugly, but at least I wasn't kicking the ball away into traffic.

You gotta get stronger. Those heavier, older girls are gonna bat you around like a beach ball. Work with some weights. Ride a bike. Heck, haul laundry up and down the stairs for a half hour at a time. Just don't sit around playing those blasted video games all day.

Carrying bags of grain and bales of hay made my muscles ache. A lot cheaper than the burn that my sister paid thirty bucks a month to get at the gym.

You gotta stutter on that layup, gal. You're too easy to time.

I had a long way to go on that one. Once I got my body moving, it was hard to pause. I worked on my left-handed hook, laughing as I flung shots way over the backboard.

"Hey, Hotshot."

Marc juggled two plates overflowing with food with a mega water bottle filled with what looked like a protein shake.

My heart thundered. Had he deliberately come looking for me? Was that what the two plates of food was about?

"Hey," I said. Brilliant opening.

"I've been meaning to ask you something."

"Yeah?" I took an easy shot, missed. Stupid.

He set down his plates on the bench, slogged his drink. "What's Savvy short for?"

I tucked the ball under my arm and turned to face him. Smile warmly, I told myself. Pretend he's just a friend like Gonzo and not the most amazing guy in the known universe and beyond. Find something amusing to say, something cute to make him laugh and those blue eyes crinkle behind those black lashes.

"Tell you what," I said. "If you tell me why you have enough food to end world hunger, I'll tell you what Savvy is short for."

Please say you brought me a plate too. That you knew the best place to find me was right here, at the hoop. That this is the best place for you too.

He grinned, showing that dimple on the right corner of his mouth. "It's all about getting bigger, Hotshot. I'm barely pushing one ninety. If I can get to an even two twenty by my senior year, I'll get into a D-1 school. That means Div—"

"I know what it means. Sheesh."

"I guess you would. They start us early, aiming for the big scholarship. Hey, you hungry? Want some food?"

"Maybe a little taste of that pork," I said.

Marc waved me over to the bench, handed me one of the plates. I plopped a hunk of pork between a roll, took a bite, and promptly dripped grease down my shirt.

He laughed and bounced his shoulder against mine. "You still owe me an answer."

I waved my sandwich in his face. "Yes, I'm hungry. Can't you tell?"

He rolled his eyes. "The Savvy thing?"

"Oh." *Stupid, stupid.* "Savannah."

"Ah. Nice."

"I suppose."

"What's Callie short for?"

"Sorry, dude. Everyone in the family has been threatened with dismemberment if we tell."

"It can't be that bad."

"I like her real name, but she hates it. So I don't get to tell."

Marc leaned back, his arms behind his head. Was he flexing or were his biceps really that tight at rest? "Tell you what. Let's go one-on-one. If I win, you have to tell me."

"You mean HORSE?"

"No. I mean one-on-one. Honestly, Hotshot—I've wanted to do this since we started hanging together on the town courts."

"Why?"

Marc leaned so close, I could smell the coleslaw on his breath. "Because I suspect you might be able to beat me."

"And that doesn't bother you?"

"It jazzes me."

"What do I get if I win?"

"Winning is enough for you," he said. "Am I right?"

"Not."

"I am. I can see it in your eyes."

"If you get something," I said, "I should too."

"You beat me, Hotshot, and I'll give you a kiss."

My heart almost erupted out of my chest and onto his potato salad. "Why would I want a kiss from a dumb football player?"

He brushed the tip of my nose with his lips. "Beat me and you'll find out."

"Whatever," I said. "Game on."

CHAPTER NINETEEN

Gonzo went over the rules, taking her job as referee seriously. "What're you guys playing to?"

"Twenty-one," Marc and I said in unison.

"Hey," he said. "Great minds."

"We'll see about that one."

Marc won the coin flip—actually, an onion chip—and got first possession. As he brought the ball in, I set in a one-man zone rather than the usual playground press. He loved spinning layups, so my plan was to keep him outside the lane.

He sunk an easy three-pointer. Worth only one point according to driveway rules but it was a beauty.

Gonzo flipped me the ball. I took it in and Marc was on me in a flash. His face a foot away from mine flustered me. I had a brain fart and almost passed to Gonzo.

I feinted right and went left. Marc didn't buy it. He kept with me all the way. I dribbled around, keeping my hip between him and the ball. I drove for the basket, fully aware of the risk of getting the ball stuffed back in my face.

Callie would freak if I embarrassed her by getting my nose broken at her party. Tough. I'd have fun my way and she could have it her way.

When I broke left, Marc hesitated, expecting to get juked. By the time I hit the basket, he was a step behind.

We played for about fifteen minutes, trading baskets back and forth. Like a real game, he bumped me under the basket. Unlike a real game, I had to keep from collapsing into his arms with an utterly girlie and absolutely stupid sigh.

I was ahead 12–10 when Marc called a time-out. He whipped off his shirt and wiped the sweat off his chest with a couple of napkins.

I thought I was going to die on the spot.

"You do some serious lifting, huh?" Gonzo said.

"I'm working at it," Marc said. "I'm too tall to be a Marvin Harrison type wideout, so I need to bulk up, get into Terrell Owens territory."

"And how do you do that?" I said.

"A really comprehensive program of weight lifting. I even do yoga and Pilates," Marc said. "Plus, good nutrition, all that health class blah blah. Whaddya say, Hotshot? Ready?"

He went back to the court, his shirt still off. Behind his back, Gonzo fluttered her hand over her heart.

After twenty minutes, the score was 20–19, his favor. I wanted to win so badly, my skin ached.

I took the ball in, driving as if for the lane, then cut right. Marc stole the ball and I cursed myself for being so predictable.

He whirled, jumped, and—

—I flew in and stuffed the shot. We scrambled for the ball. I got there first, and before he could extend his arms, I jumped, shot, and *swish*.

"Game point," Gonzo called out.

Marc inbounded and drove for the middle of the lane. He

jumped and deked sideways. I flailed, tipping the ball just enough to deflect it against the rim.

I came down with the rebound. He tried to grab the ball away, whipping it—and me—around so hard, I fell.

"Foul!" Gonzo called.

"No way," Marc said. "I had the ball. She should have let go. Or you should have whistled the play."

"If I say foul, it's a foul. Or do you want me to toss you?"

Marc passed me the ball. "Next time one of *my* friends refs."

I stood at the free throw line, bouncing the ball. This was a money shot for me.

"You ain't makin' this shot, baby," Marc whispered. "You're too pretty to make this shot."

Trash talk was a staple of the game, but no one had ever sweet-talked me before. I shot and—*bang!*—rattled the rim.

I leaped high, my hands stretching over Marc's. He jammed me with his shoulder and, even though I had the ball, I couldn't keep it. He dribbled out to the circle, turned, and shot.

Swish.

"Thanks for the game, sweet cheeks." Marc wrapped his arms around my waist and lifted me off the ground. "Pay up, baby. Tell me what Callie is short for."

I pushed away, pretending my blood wasn't rushing so hard, it was about to shoot out my ears. "Just don't tell her who told you."

He pressed my hand to his mouth. "My lips are sealed."

"Her name is Calliope," I said.

"Okay, good enough. I'll torment her with it next time I see her. I'm gonna go up to your house, get cleaned up in the kitchen. Your parents won't mind, will they?"

"No."

"Hey ladies, this has been a lot of fun. Thanks, Hotshot, and you too, Gonz."

He grabbed his shirt and ran up the driveway, his form so perfect, I expected him to keep running straight into heaven.

Gonzo dapped me. "Hey. Good game. You coming back to the party now?"

"I'm going up to the house. I need a shower."

"You go, girl. I'll catch you when you come back down."

"Yeah. Sure," I said. "Wish me luck."

"You don't need luck, Hotshot. You got game."

O=-O=-O=-O=-

Marc slipped out the back door of the house just as I came in the front. I wanted to glom on to him but I needed to wash off the game sweat and put on my party sweet. I ran upstairs, took a thirty-second shower, changed my clothes, tried to redo my makeup, and then wandered over to the barn.

Gonzo said he had come into the barn, grabbed a soda, and disappeared. "Maybe he's back out with the kids driving golf balls. Want me to come with you to find him?"

"No, I got this," I said.

I finally spotted Marc up in the birches by the high pasture. I shook out my hair, straightened my tank top, and checked my breath. Just go, I thought. He wouldn't be up by the sheep if he wasn't different from any other guy I had ever met.

If he wasn't so totally, amazingly special.

I walked up the dirt road, losing sight of him halfway up. It would be cool under the birches, a nice place to talk.

Coming around the curve of the road, I saw that Marc had drifted deeper into the trees. His tropical print shirt flashed yellow and blue in the cool shade.

Visualize the shot, I thought. Think about what it could be like. As Fitz said, *practice success*.

I could see it so easily. Next weekend was the high school's first football game. The band would play and Marc would be on the sidelines, jumping with his teammates to get psyched up. He'd spot me in the stands and give me a little wave. Later he might tell me how nice it was I was tall—like a model—so he could always find me.

The game would start, the other team acting like tanks and missiles on the field. Marc would dart through, a gazelle among bulls. The quarterback would unleash a pass—too high and off-target—but he would stretch with long fingers, snare the ball, and throw himself into the end zone.

The guys would chest-butt him but even from far away, his eyes would search out mine. I'd smile and press my fist to my heart.

Like any of that could ever happen.

Practice success, Fitz said, his nagging so persistent that it reached even to the high pasture.

I hopped over the fence, pretending to check on the sheep. Manny ran to me, took a sniff, and went back in the shade.

The sheep grazed quietly, not at all interested in what I might be doing. I took one by the scruff so her odor wouldn't rub off on me and curled back her ears to check them. Gonzo, the superstar of drama queens, would be impressed by my performance.

It would look genuine to Marc, like I wasn't following him but just taking care of business. I glanced over my shoulder and saw that unfortunately, he hadn't caught a moment of it. He had strayed deeper into the birches.

Take the shot or take the bench, I thought.

I hopped back over the fence and wandered after him. Aunt Betty had me mow under the birch trees to keep the underbrush down. The grass muffled the sound of my footsteps, which was why Marc never turned to look as I approached.

That—and the fact that he was wrapped around Callie, his tongue searching for her tonsils.

CHAPTER TWENTY

The first day of school was blazing hot. I pulled on a pale-peach sleeveless top and matched it with a mid-thigh denim skirt.

"Killer outfit," Callie said. She looked spectacular in tight jeans and a red silk tee-shirt. She'd be starting high school on top—a hot-looking cheerleader with a heart-breaking boyfriend.

I didn't want to talk to her, couldn't stand even looking at her. I didn't know who I hated more. Marc, for using me to get in with Callie—or Callie, because I had killed myself for her party and she came away with the prize.

I had been so stupid to think any guy—let alone the world's most spectacular—would want a girl as big as me.

"Savvy, you all right?"

The last thing I wanted was the world's most pitiful daughter to show pity on me. "I'm fine. You have a cold? You're all raspy again."

"Allergies again. Have a good one, Savvy." Callie shouldered her pack. She didn't even have to take the bus today. Marc was picking her up.

The bus for the middle school arrived forty-five minutes later. Gonzo lived across town, so I didn't know a soul. I slouched into a seat and pretended to be short.

Walking into Taylor Middle School for the first time was

the nightmare I knew it would be. The stupid sixth-grade boys poked each other, made dumb jokes. Some idiot kid walked alongside me, jumping like a kangaroo, trying to get into my face. Gonzo rescued me, taking me into the eighth-grade wing. Boys stared openly and girls whispered to each other—so glad not to be a freak like the new girl.

As bad luck would have it, I had no classes with Gonzo. She promised to meet me at lunch and introduce me around. *She's really tall,* she was probably telling kids to prepare them. *But she's cool.*

The questions started in homeroom and continued all morning. Not one person asked where I came from. It was all: *How tall are you? How old are you?* And, of course: *Do you play basketball?*

By tomorrow my fellow eighth graders would be bored with me. I just had to endure the next six hours and fourteen minutes. Lunch was the high point. I sat with Gonzo and her friends Jamie and Leah. They were pointing out all the cute guys in our grade and warning me about the jerks—as if I hadn't already met them—when we got interrupted by some blond girl.

"Are you Savvy?"

"Yeah."

"I'm Alyssa's sister, Maddie. She told me to be sure to say hi today."

"Oh."

"She said you're going to do some modeling. That's really cool."

"Um . . . yeah, maybe. Nothing's set up."

"I'm only five six but hoping to grow another four inches, then give it a try. You're lucky. They're desperate for girls over six feet."

"I guess."

"Well, have a great day." Maddie made her way across the room to what had to be the popular kids, based on all the envious looks she got as she passed.

Leah leaned across the table. "You're gonna model?"

"No. I mean, I don't know. I mean, who knows? Maybe."

"Wow," she said. "Wow."

Lunch was pretty good after that. Gonzo introduced kids. I got a lot of questions about New Mexico and my father's golfing career. The afternoon moved like a slug but somehow I made it to the last class of the day, world history. Mrs. Potter passed out what she called an assessment.

"No fair," some dork behind me shouted out. "You're quizzing us already?"

"Apparently you don't know what the word *assessment* means."

"I know what it means."

"Look it up anyway." She plopped a dictionary on his desk, then turned to the rest of us. "The point of this non-graded test is to determine if you have any knowledge of the world beyond *Pirates of the Caribbean* and *Spider-Man*."

I bent over my paper, trying to get through the first block of multiple choices. I had no clue about the Spanish Inquisition or the War of 1812. The only thing I knew about Castro's Cuba was that baseball players braved sharks and hurricanes to paddle to the United States. Trade with China meant Yao Ming. The fall of the Soviet Union brought a rush of talent into the NHL and the NBA from eastern Europe.

Clearly, these questions were Greek to most of us. Some kids put their heads down and napped. Others opened cell phones no one was supposed to have and texted. I watched the clock and thought, Another eighteen minutes and the first day of school will be in the record books.

The custodian knocked at the door. Mrs. Potter went out into the hall for a chat. More like an argument—something about the lights not working in this room.

I did my best to get through the geography section. The Caribbean meant David Ortiz while the Mediterranean was a place where rich people partied on yachts. Argentina was Manu Ginóbili and New Zealand was a place I wanted to go ever since *The Lord of the Rings*. Antarctica was too cold for any fool to go, if you asked me, but "O Canada," because they had given us Steve Nash.

When I was a WNBA superstar, he and I would go one-on-one, maybe to raise money for charity or something. The notion of stuffing Nash was good for five minutes of daydreaming.

Something bounced against my arm. A folded note plopped on the floor. I knew better than to pick it up.

I went on with the quiz-that-wasn't-a-quiz, thinking how stupid it was to ask kids our age about the caste system in India. You want caste, check out your local middle school. Being bigger than everyone had somehow made me less than everyone.

A paper plane wafted onto my desk. The message would be some variation on the *Ho, ho, ho jolly girl giant* or *What freak show did you escape from.* Did the snorting boys behind me think they had material I hadn't heard before?

"Open it," someone hissed.

I turned around to see two boys smirking at me. One had a buzz cut and a mouth full of braces—the jerk who didn't know what assessment meant. The other was a fish-faced moron who flexed his nonexistent bicep at me. Bad enough I had to be teased. Couldn't my tormentors at least be good-looking?

"Come on, virago," Buzz Cut said. "Check it out."

I didn't like the sound of *virago,* but no way would I ask to borrow the dictionary to look it up. Sometimes it's better not to know.

Before I had a chance to whiz the note back to them, Mrs. Potter came into the room. She collected our quizzes, passed out our books, and assigned us homework. I slid the note into my backpack and walked to the bus, my head held high.

I sat in the back seat and opened the note.

Hey there. U on the juice?

I looked at my reflection in the window. A month of hard farm work had bulked up my shoulders and arms. The change had come so slowly, I hadn't really noticed until some idiot loser tagged me with the steroid thing.

Stupid sleeveless top. Stupid middle school.

High school was one long, ugly year away.

When I got home, there was a strange car in the driveway. The visiting nurse, I assumed. She came once a day to help Aunt Betty shower. That drove my aunt nuts, but until she got that cast off, a helping hand was better than cracking her head and going back into the hospital.

I ran up the stairs to change my shirt, determined to wear long sleeves for the rest of my life. Or at least until I was such a star that no one would make fun of me.

Marc Sardakis was in my closet, digging around on the floor. "Hey, Hotshot."

"What're you doing here?" I said.

"Your sister forgot her sneakers. I said I'd drive her home before practice."

"Where is she?"

"The bathroom. Wow, you look pissed." He stood, his eyes locked on mine. "Did I do something wrong?"

Raise my hopes, break my heart, humiliate me—and then rub it in by dating my sister? "No, I'm not pissed," I said. "Why would I be? What do you need in the closet?"

"I said I'd grab the sneakers while Callie peed. But I can't find them."

I stepped around him, trying not to touch him. His breath was hot on my face and his shampoo smelled masculine and sexy. He wore cool jeans and a black T-shirt just snug enough to show off his pecs.

A blush rose up my neck, a raw fury with the universe that decreed that just because Callie was a foot shorter than me, she got the hot boyfriend and I got the stupid note from a mouth-breathing snot.

I shoved aside my basketball bag and found Callie's sneakers. "Here," I said, turning—

—and bumping right into Marc. We were nose to nose for a long moment until Callie came in.

"Did you get them?" she said.

No *Hi Sav, how was school today, hope it all went well for you.*

"Yeah," Marc said. "Come on, we gotta book it."

They were halfway down the stairs when I called my sister back up.

"What? I'm in a hurry," she said.

"You know the rules," I said. "We're not supposed to have guys in our room. Or even in the house if Mom and Dad aren't home."

"I was just getting my sneakers. You got a problem with that?"

"I don't appreciate coming home and finding a stranger in my room, that's all."

"You gonna snitch to Mom and Dad again?"

Marc beeped from down in the driveway.

"Why should I care about what you do?" I said. "Just leave me out of it."

CHAPTER TWENTY-ONE

September was all about school, and school was all about jerks and homework. I could ignore the jerks most of the time, but homework meant squeezing time in for Manny and the sheep. Though she was still in a cast, Aunt Betty did as much as she could, which wasn't a heck of a lot.

Every once in a while, my parents would offer to help, but with what time? Mom got home late every night and Dad spent long hours studying. And as if their time wasn't stretched enough, my parents were now buddies with all the football players and cheerleaders, and the first game of the season was a must-see.

"You should tell them to stay home," I said to Callie. "They're worn out."

"You gonna tell them to stay home from your tournament this weekend?"

"That's different. I play out of town, so I need them to drive."

"No," Callie said. "You need your number one fans."

"Like you don't?"

Callie smiled. "Not anymore."

If my sister's life was suddenly perfect, it was only because all the rest of us had made it that way. She turns a couple of cartwheels, flashes a cheerleader grin, and bang! She was *in*.

A couple weeks after school started, Fire had its usual

Thursday night practice. After an hour of drills, Fitz called a break. I downed a bottle of water and a cupcake.

"Empty calories," Lori said.

I ignored her. No way could I ignore Bailey when she said, "Can you dunk yet, Savvy?"

"Yeah, sure." Not that I ever had.

"You're lying. I'll bet a meatball grinder that you can't."

"What size?"

"Usual," Bailey said.

"Make it a foot-long. And you're on."

"Gambling is illegal," Lori said. "And undignified."

Bailey glared at her. "We're just horsing around. Don't make a federal case out of it."

"When?" I asked.

"Now." Fitz always left us alone for our fifteen-minute break. Team building, he said, but we thought he might be sneaking smokes with the janitor.

Bailey and I settled on ten tries to get it done. Everyone, except Lori, came down onto the floor to watch.

"Where do you want me to feed you the ball from?" Gonzo asked.

"Stand on the baseline, hit me on the right side. On the middle block."

On the first seven tries, I was able to tip the ball at the edge of the rip, spinning it off my fingertips, but I couldn't get my hand actually above the rim. Each time I came down, the gym floor thundered from my weight. I had gained almost fifteen pounds but still wore the same pants size.

Muscles, Mom said when I mentioned this. Not fair, Callie whined.

Fitz came in from his break and saw us. He narrowed his eyes at me, turned, and walked back out.

"Try from the front," Gonzo said, even though she knew I hated approaching the basket straight on.

I took a few jumps and ruffled the net, trying to find a good launch spot. I backed up, took a running start from the top of the key. Gonzo hit me perfectly with the pass.

I smashed the ball into the rim, almost decapitating myself with the bounce-back. Gonzo rolled on the floor with laughter.

"Stop it," Lori said. "You're all acting stupid. Someone's going to get hurt."

Screw her with her rules that stunk and her sweat that didn't. I'd show her.

"I'm taking it from the left side," I said.

"Oh man," Bailey said. "Everyone stand back."

"I don't want a bounce pass. Just a regular pass, chest high."

"You want me to toss it up so you can push it in?" Gonzo asked.

"No. I'm taking it up myself. Just hit me with it and leave the rest to me." I jogged around for a few seconds to loosen up.

Me, the ball, and the basket. Nothing else in the world.

No Marc or Callie or coyotes or stupid Buzz Cut or Goggles or Lori—even though she stared down on me from the bleachers like she was God.

Focus all over again.

Me. I ran down the left side of the key.

Ball. In my hands, rising with me.

Basket. Eye-to-eye with me.

Me. Still rising, the ball part of my skin, flying up until I was higher than I'd ever been.

In a hard, wonderful, amazing push—I dunked the ball.

My teammates whooped and hollered. Bailey hugged me, not caring she had lost the bet. Gonzo muttered something about getting half the grinder since she did half the work. I let them pound on me, numb and silent.

Because my feet still hadn't touched the ground.

○=○=○=○=

A minute later, Fitz motioned me out to the hall. "What the blazes was that, Christopher?"

"Um . . . just trying to dunk."

"Dunk. And risk breaking your ankle. Or twisting your knee. Real smart, gal."

My blood, still hot from the dunk, boiled over. "So why didn't you tell me to stop?"

Fitz tugged on his shaggy eyebrow. "Because I wanted to see if you could do it."

"I did. So now what?"

"So don't do it again. Stick with the plan."

Stick with the plan. I was sick to death of taking a grubby sheet home from every practice with his plan. Then again, his plan was probably a big part of me stuffing the ball down the basket's throat.

We went back in, circled around for scrimmage. Lori gave

me a smug look, pleased that I had gotten a talking to.

Fitz pulled out the pinnies, tossed one to Molly, another to Bailey. By the time he handed Gonzo hers, Olivia and I were already whispering about what zone we'd pull against them.

"Christopher."

"Huh?" I looked up.

With a face as stern as a barbed wire fence, Fitz tossed me a pinny. "Center."

I was so surprised, I didn't even try to catch it. Bailey flipped it onto my lap with a whispered, "Way to go."

No bells, no drums, no chorus singing *hallelujahs*. Just a faded orange pinny to signal my move to starter for the 18U Kent County Fire.

I thought I'd leap over the basket and never come down.

OCTOBER

CHAPTER TWENTY-TWO

Okay, maybe Rhode Island wasn't so bad after all.

The oaks, maples, and birches had changed from green to smoldering yellow, smoky gold, blazing red against deep blue skies. The days were still warm but the nights made us shiver. One morning, I woke up to find the grass glittering white. An early frost, Dad said.

Though school had started and the tournament season was in full swing, I kept up with chasing sheep, repairing fences, lugging hay bales. Every day I pushed Aunt Betty up the long road to the high pasture, working out my quads and calves. Coming down was all about my arms and hamstrings because I had to keep the wheelchair from going airborne.

The first weekend in October, Mr. Otis sent over a wagon of hay. Once the grass was gone, each sheep would need about four pounds of hay a day. In New England, the pastures would be snowed or iced under for over a hundred days. Each bale weighed forty pounds.

The math was scary. The wagon load was only the first of many that would come. Aunt Betty and Mr. Otis planned to shuffle the hay into the hay shed. Sheesh, between them they were a century and a half old.

"No way," I said. "I want to do it."

They didn't argue long. Mom gave the two of them passes

to the Warwick Fair that a customer had given her. They left bright and early, planning to party until dark with award-winning pumpkins and fat-bottomed cattle.

Wow, what a killer date.

Fire had three games on Saturday, so I didn't get to the job until after supper. The sun was low in the west, making the trees seem to catch fire. The chipmunks scurried on rock walls, twittering for acorns. From the high pasture, a sheep bleated.

"Wear long pants and socks," Aunt Betty had warned. "There's poison ivy all around the hay shed."

Too hot, even this late in the day. I'd wash my legs good when I was done. Besides, I had never had poison ivy in my life.

I was about to start the job when Manny barked from the high pasture. Crap, I thought.

I hiked up the road, spotted Manny in the northeast corner of the pasture, barking at the birches.

Freakin' coyotes. I ran into trees, screaming, "Go away, you scumbags. Just go!"

Marc and Callie jumped up from a blanket, red-faced and sweaty. She straightened her shirt and cursed me out.

My head felt like it was going to explode. I could easily rip her head off her shoulders. Instead, I took a long, deep breath. And I gave her the finger.

"You wish," Callie shouted. "You so wish, Savvy."

"Ladies," Marc said. "Calm down."

Too late—my sister had launched herself at me like a howling cat. A good ten inches taller than her, I grabbed her and shoved her at Marc.

"She's your problem now," I said. "Enjoy."

I went into the house to eat something—anything—that would get rid of the ache in my belly. I'd unload the hay later, once I got the image of my sister and Marc out of my head.

My father sat at the kitchen table, his head in his hands.

"You okay?" I said.

He jolted, his eyes heavy-lidded. "Must have dozed off."

"But are you okay?"

"Yes. No. I don't know. I got a C minus on my microeconomics exam."

"Oh man, that stinks."

He slipped on his reading glasses, went back to his book. "Not for you to worry about, Savvy."

I grabbed a hunk of oatmeal bread and sat down with him. "You got B's in your summer stuff. So you'll be okay in this."

"I know. But it's the getting there that just . . . I don't know . . ."

"Sucks?"

"Yeah." My father rubbed his eyes. "Sucks."

"But you do get there, Daddy. You think you won't get it done, but you do."

He got up, stretched. "I need a cup of coffee."

I went back out into the field, wishing I could give him something beyond *it sucks*.

I got into a nice rhythm unloading the bales. Lift, carry, stack—a backbreaking job that Aunt Betty had been doing since the tender age of sixty-three when she retired from teaching to work the farm full-time.

Lift, carry, stack—can't think about Marc and Callie.

Lift, carry, stack—my muscles warming to the task even as the first star winked on over the trees.

Lift, carry, stack—jump, shoot, *swish*—I would be like this forever.

Lift, carry, stack—drop the hay, stop and sit.

Sit and cry my stupid eyes out. Not because of Callie and Marc. They weren't worth one drop, not in this moment when I suddenly understood what my father had lost. Not just a great golf career but a thousand simple things that most of us take for granted. Pounding a board. Lifting a bag of groceries. Picking up a lamb. No wonder he had resisted having the surgery. No wonder Mom had let him keep trying to get back to golf even as pain gripped his body and our money drained away.

When you love someone, you can't deny them their dream, even when you know it's long gone.

I ran across the low pasture, down the drive, across the lawn—grateful that I could.

Dad was in the kitchen, finishing his coffee. I gave him the sweatiest, smelliest, most awesome hug ever.

"What's that for?" he said, laughing.

"Because," I said. "Just because."

CHAPTER TWENTY-THREE

The high point of the SBA season was the national tournament in Orlando over Thanksgiving vacation. The only way a team could play in it was to win a regional qualifier.

The first qualifier in New England was held in Warwick over Columbus Day weekend. Fire intended to win, since no one wanted to travel out of state over Veteran's Day weekend to try again.

"We got this one locked," Gonzo promised.

I believed her. We had won the jamboree, plus two of the three tournaments we played in September. Gonzo said we would have won the third if I didn't go down with a wicked case of strep throat and a 103-degree fever. I believed her on that one too.

Not that I was arrogant. On the score sheet, I'd rather see a *W* next to Fire than *30 points/12 rebounds* next to Christopher. Even so, it was cool that Gonzo and I—the two youngest kids—now started for Fire. Fitz had been diplomatic about it, made sure that Lori got lots of playing time. But when we took the court on Friday night, Gonzo was at point guard and I was at center.

After breezing through the first game, we had a tough one Saturday morning with a team from Lowell, Massachusetts. The weeping poison-ivy rash on my ankles drove me nuts. It was so bad, the doctor had prescribed prednisone pills. Aunt Betty had warned me to wear long pants when I unloaded the hay. If I hadn't been such a jerk about not listening to her, I wouldn't have to be so grown-up now and resist an itch so bad, I wanted to scratch all the way to my bones.

Fitz played the bench in the second game on Saturday against a Connecticut team. We had a comfortable lead through the whole game. Lori threw nervous glances my way, expecting me to come in for her. I cheered her on, trying to be a good teammate.

I had a misty moment when I wondered if somehow I had taken Lori's *one thing* from her. I didn't want to damage her. I just wanted to do my best. That's what competition was about.

We were scheduled to play Power in our last game of the day. Both teams had won three games and whoever lost the game would still make the elimination round. But that wasn't the point.

Establishing dominance was.

For supper, my parents ate sandwiches out of a cooler. They let me run into the local Burger Shack to buy a couple of quarter-pounders. "And for heaven's sake, Savvy," Mom said. "Don't scratch that poison ivy. You know the blood rule—you bleed, you sit until you're patched up."

I stood in a crowd, studying the menu.

Jennifer Kronos appeared out of nowhere. "So what looks good here?"

"Um . . . everything." She made me so nervous, I started to scratch my ankles.

"How's the tournament treating you, Savvy?"

"Okay. You?"

"Don't tell anyone, but . . . so far it's been boring. I'm looking forward to tonight's game. Some real competition."

The line began to move. Servers had been called to the front to handle the tournament crowd.

"You been working out some, Savvy?"

"Not really."

She tilted her head, studied me. "You've put on some muscle. And that's a good thing these days."

"I work around my aunt's farm. It was either that or . . ." I surprised myself by spilling my guts about the whole thing. Coyotes. Aunt Betty's bad luck. Fixing fences, repairing the hay shed, lifting bales of hay and bags of grain.

Kronos nodded as if I were telling her I had come up with an end to war, world hunger, and Shaq's free throw woes.

"Can I help you?" the counter girl asked.

"Oh. Sorry." I gave my order and stepped aside to wait.

After asking for a large coffee, Kronos took out a ten-dollar bill. "Hers is on me too," she said.

"Oh no, that's all right." I looked around, worried Fitz would see us.

"It's not a bribe. Just a thank-you for keeping me company while we waited in this silly line." She sipped her coffee. "By the way, I'm sure you know that the AAU season begins in December. If you're looking for a team, the offer still stands. We'd love to have you."

I clicked my fingernails together, weighing the option. Kronos and Pat Summit on the plus side, Goggles and dirty play on the minus side.

"I don't know."

"Is Fitz treating you okay?"

"Yeah, I guess. Why?"

"He's been known to go over the line."

Talk about the sheep calling the goat full of crap. "You're kidding, right?"

Kronos shook her head, her eyes locked on mine. "No, I'm not."

"You don't think you go over the line, with the way your team plays so rough?" I asked.

"My team doesn't play rough. We play grown-up."

"Yeah, okay. If you say so."

Kronos shrugged. "We'll talk later, Savvy. Good luck tonight."

"Wait. Why do you want me on your team so bad?"

"Because I know you'll go to Tennessee or UCONN or Rutgers or wherever you choose. And I want to be the coach who'll get you there."

She gave me another one of those *aren't-we-just-the-best-of-buddies* winks and left.

CHAPTER TWENTY-FOUR

We warmed up at our side of the court, trying to hit every shot. No fooling around, no missing passes, all business. Intimidation through perfection is a great strategy for winning.

"They will fear us," Bailey said. "Why will they fear us?"

We chanted in whispers that were far more chilling than if we shouted. *We press, we rebound, we shoot, we score.*

"They will respect us," Molly said. "Why will they respect us?"

We play hard, we play tough, we never give up.

"Remember why we beat them back in August," Bubble said.

We beat them because Goggles only played half the game, I thought. But I kept my whisper going: *We press, we rebound . . .* After warm-ups, I excused myself to go to the locker room. Gonzo followed me. "What's up with you? You look like your face is going to explode."

"I'm going nuts, trying not to scratch. I'm afraid if anyone finds out about"—I pulled my sock away, showed her the pus-filled rash that was my poison ivy—"they won't let me play. I'm on steroids for it. But . . ."

"Hey. Secret's safe with me."

I unlocked my basket, gooped more cream onto the rash. The warning buzzer blew and we flew out to the floor. Gonzo gave Fitz the one answer for being late that always got us off the hook. "Time of the month, Coach."

We won the coin flip and got first possession. Bubble took the ball out, looked for me on the sideline. I slammed a pass to Molly at the top of the key and followed it in, yelling, "Me!"

All a ruse to draw Goggles out of the paint to take me on. Molly hit Bubble mid-chest with the pass. She went up for the shot. A girl who looked like a string bean deflected it.

I flew in for the rebound, Goggles right with me. We landed in a heap, fighting over the ball. Neither of us let go until the whistle blew. As she got up, she elbowed me in the gut.

Thirty seconds into the game and already we were at war.

"What is your problem?" I said.

"You, freak-face. But you won't get away with it this time."

"Get away with what?"

"Stealing the"—she cut in a choice swear word—"game."

"Don't have to steal what we already own."

For the next few possessions, both teams played tight defense, keeping shooters out of the paint. I tried to get in the low post but Goggles outweighed and out-toughed me. I needed room to shoot.

Fitz called time, put Lori in at center and moved me to forward. "Feed Christopher and then get inside, Penske," he said. "If they double her, she'll pass under. Christopher, you have my permission to go for any outside shots you think you can hit. Got it?"

We broke, took possession. I set up in high post. I felt a

little pang that I had just displaced Bailey from her position. Hopefully, she'd forgive me.

When action resumed, I spun away from Goggles. Lori stepped in to screen so Goggles had to either swerve or foul. The girl might be an animal but she wasn't stupid—she stepped around Lori, losing three steps on me.

Bubble inbounded to Gonzo. She fed me at the baseline. I drained my favorite shot and collected three sweet points for Fire.

"They're gonna double-down on you now," Gonzo whispered as she dapped my fist.

Double-team on me meant someone would always be in the clear. We scored three easy baskets. Gonzo got one, Molly sank two. With us up by five points, Kronos called time.

"Don't get cocky because we're ahead," Fitz growled. "This is a smart team."

"How 'bout that—apes have evolved some intelligence," Gonzo whispered.

A Power guard took the ball in, shuffling it to String Bean at the baseline. She glanced Goggles's way. Before the ball had even left her hands, I started my spring. As I came back down with the steal, something hit me between the shoulder blades.

My face slammed against the floor—time slowing so I could see tiny grains of sand on the hardwood. I bounced, hit again and rolled to take it on my shoulder.

The ball was still in play. Gonzo raced after it but couldn't get it before it went out of bounds. Only then did the whistle blow.

I glared at the ref. "Didn't you see that? I was shoved."

"Sorry, Fire," she said. "Can't call something I didn't see."

"Son of—how could you miss that?"

Bubble pulled me away. "Power's trying to set you up to get you tossed," she said. "Chill."

Chill? I wanted to rip someone's face off. The tightness in my cheek meant a bruise was blooming. Lovely—I was enough of a freak at Taylor Middle School without showing up Tuesday all black and blue.

Fire set up in zone, Goggles bumping me with her hip. "Had enough yet?"

"Bring it on, maggot," I said. "Bring it on."

O=O=O=O=

Basketball is a physical game. In the NBA, it can be a brutal game. But there's no reason why it should be a dirty game. I wasn't afraid of contact, but I was furious at being smacked and shoved every time the referees weren't looking.

Molly said the Newport Power team was made up of rich girls, most of whom went to private school and liked to play at being tough. Instead of tea and crumpets, Goggles and her thugs served up a brawl. Did Kronos condone this? She yelled at the two players who'd already fouled out like she meant it.

But Power just kept dealing the pain and the officials kept missing it.

As we approached the half, Goggles backed off. She was on her third foul and too valuable to her team to leave early. When Fitz realized she was giving me space, he moved me back to center. Lori went to the bench, staring poison at the world.

String Bean passed to Goggles as she moved into the paint. I stayed with her, going up as she leaped to shoot. As I slapped the ball away, she elbowed my arm, recoiling as if I had whacked her.

Tweet! "Foul on Fire, twenty-three."

"You have got to be kidding!" I said.

"Friggin' faker," Gonzo hissed.

The ref motioned Goggles to the foul line. Ready to go postal, I gave in to the one urge I could relieve without getting called for a technical. I scratched my poison ivy—hard. I raked my fingernails up and down, and my blisters felt good for a moment before itching even worse. Goggles made the first foul shot, smiled at me, and mouthed *thanks*.

As she took the ball for the second one, String Bean pointed at me. "Hey, she's bleeding."

Crap. I had scratched through the blisters and bloodied my sock. I'd have to sub out until I changed. Lori came in for me. I grabbed gauze out of the first aid kit and ran into the locker room.

Screw tradition—with no clean socks in my bag, I had to dig into my trophies. I unzipped that compartment, grabbed last week's socks, and left everything in a jumble. I locked up my basket and raced back to the game.

Goggles was on the bench. We'd both played the entire first half without a rest. Kronos must have used my absence as an opportunity to rest her enforcer.

Sweet. My first year in this league and I was already a marked player.

CHAPTER TWENTY-FIVE

At halftime, the score was Fire 22, Power 19.

Girls scattered to go to the bathroom, get drinks, splash water on their faces. I stayed on the bench so that Mom could wrap my ankles. She lectured me about the dirty socks but hey—maybe last week's tournament win would carry over.

Before play resumed, Fitz gathered us around to go through our foul status. Lori had been a Girl Scout all game—she was the only Fire player with no fouls. Someone needed to take sandpaper to her and toughen her up.

"They're breaking rules left and right," Lori said. "No one is doing anything about it."

Fitz frowned. "Penske, I just told you we're in much better shape than they are in regard to fouls."

"They play rough."

"No, they play grown-up," he said.

Kronos had said the same thing to me two hours ago.

"We're playing in a game of attrition," Fitz said. "Last one standing wins. Play hard, play clean. And gals—you have got to believe that the rules count for something. The officials can't see everything, and this crew is pretty nearsighted. But as this stinkin' Power team grows more desperate, they'll get so sloppy, the refs can't ignore them. When that happens, they'll lose their starters to foul trouble as fast as I lose my hair."

We laughed, circled around for *1-2-3-play tough,* and broke.

Fitz started me at center. Bailey and Olivia were in as forwards, Ava and Gonzo at guard. Lori sat on the bench, her head in her hands.

The teams traded back-and-forth baskets. Gonzo intercepted a pass, and as she went for the fast break, String Bean's foot just happened to get in the way. The whistle blew and String Bean was out of the game with her fifth foul.

Gonzo pushed up slowly from the floor, her nose dripping with blood. Goggles snickered. Olivia subbed into the game, handed Gonzo a towel. I watched her walk off, head back, staring fury at the ceiling. Grown-up play, my ass.

I'd rather grow up to be George Otis than Jennifer Kronos.

I called for time, went to the Power bench, and got in the woman's face. "What is up with you and your pit bull bitches?"

"Savvy, you shouldn't be over here," she said.

Fitz ran over, grabbed the back of my shirt. "Get out of here before you draw a technical."

"You're not good enough to beat us. That's why you just beat up on us."

Dad stood on the top bleacher, his face creased with worry. Molly wrapped her hand around my mouth. "Shush. We need you in the game."

I yanked out of her grasp, went back to Kronos. "Pat Summit would be ashamed."

She shook her head, lips pressed tight.

"Technical on Fire," the ref said. "Be glad it's not worse. I'll let you stay in the game, twenty-three. But no more outbursts."

"She'll behave," Fitz said. "Right?"

I nodded.

"We want clean play." The ref looked directly at me. "No taunting or outbursts. We'll give you thirty seconds on the time-out. Starting now, Fire."

Fitz pulled us in. "Heads back in the game. Gonzalez, you stopped bleeding?"

"Yes, sir." With gauze stuffed up her nose, it sounded like *Nyeah, suh*.

"Penske, back in at center. You have one task and I expect you to deliver. Keep that gorilla with the goggles off Christopher. You got me?"

Lori bit her upper lip. "Yes."

"Work the outside for the next couple of plays. Get the ball to Christopher or to Muir—let them drain a couple of threes, get us a cushion on these girls. Let's press full court on the next couple possessions, slow them down. Take the fouls and don't whine if you get a poke in the gut. Your best revenge is a turnover or a free throw. Got it?"

We nodded.

"Play your game, not theirs. Make me and your parents proud."

I glanced around the gym, trying to spot the fiends who had spawned Goggles. Mrs. Latham, the tournament director, was at the door, deep in conversation with a cop. Whaddya know, I thought. Maybe the rules really did count for something.

Maybe they're gonna haul Kronos and her dogs off to jail.

CHAPTER TWENTY-SIX

Thanks to Gonzo, the game fizzled to a dull but satisfying end.

Midway through the second half, Power put on a full-court press. Gonzo took the ball from Bubble in the back court and went on a coast-to-coast. The Power guard stayed on her but Gonzo wouldn't pass off.

I realized what she was up to when she took Goggles straight on. Gonzo took a jumper but Goggles blocked the shot easy. Easy and clean, I thought, but Gonzo flew backward, legs splayed.

The whistle blew.

"A winning performance," I said as I helped her up.

Gonzo grinned and went to the line.

Goggles went to the bench with five fouls. With Power's intimidator out of the game, we won by a hefty eight points.

Fire went into the elimination round as one of four top seeds. With one loss, Power also made the elimination round, but they were a bottom seed. My parents had disappeared from the stands. Maybe out buying me food, I hoped. As we cleaned up our bench, Mrs. Latham came over.

"There's a bit of a problem in the locker room," she said. "If you could all just sit for a few minutes."

"Can I run to the concession table and get something to eat?" I asked. "I'm starved."

"We want you just to sit here. Please." She left, the worried look on her face giving me the creepy-crawlies.

"Maybe it's a bomb threat," Molly said.

"We'd go outside then," Bailey said.

Lori clenched her hands, trying to hide the tremble in her fingers. My first thought was: *Baby*. My second thought was: *She's your teammate, jerk. Act like it.*

"Hey, Lori," I said. "Bailey's right. If there was a bomb, they'd have us out in the parking lot, our head between our knees or something dumb."

She wouldn't look at me. Grief, I could do nothing right where she was concerned.

Dad came in with Mrs. Latham, followed by Ava's mother. Ava and I stood, her face drained of color and my heart skipping beats. "This isn't about you," her mother said. "They just need someone to stay with the team."

Dad touched my shoulder. "Come along for a minute, okay?"

"Why?" My mind popped with horrible possibilities. *Car accident—kidnapping—oh dear God, rape—something horrible— not my sister, please God. Let Callie be okay. I don't really hate her—I'm sorry, God.*

Dad read my eyes and said, "We're all fine. Just come along."

O⇒O⇒O⇒O⇒

My father steered me into the office next to the girls' locker room. Mom was already there, with a woman with spiked frosted hair and sad brown eyes. My gym bag was on the desk.

"Who went in my locker?" I said.

"Savvy, sit down please," Dad said.

Frosted Hair extended her hand to me. "I'm Detective Beth Carrod. Cranston Police."

Why the heck was everyone looking at me?

"Did someone steal something from me? I don't keep money in my bag. Just water and socks. Dirty socks. Nothing else. I know better than to put anything of value in there. Even though we lock it up. There's nothing in there for someone to steal . . ."

Detective Carrod sat on the corner of the desk. "Savvy is an unusual name. What's it short for?"

"Oh for Pete's sake," Dad said. "Can we cut the small talk, please?"

"Savannah," I said. "Why do you have my gym bag?"

She ignored him, kept her gaze on me. "Do you prefer Savvy?"

"I don't care," I said. "What do you need me for?"

"Someone phoned the police to report a significant quantity of drugs in your gym bag."

My head took a light-speed spin through the Twilight Zone. "My bag? That's insane."

"We assumed it was a mistake," Mom said. "Otherwise we wouldn't have allowed them to cut open your lock and search your bag."

"We found this." Detective Carrod showed me a sandwich bag full of pills.

My skin prickled as everything telescoped in and out, like one of those out-of-the-body things. "That can't be my bag if there's stuff in there like that."

Mom squatted next to my chair, touched my hair. "It is your bag, honey."

"I understand you're a tremendous athlete," Detective Carrod said. "Sometimes vast potential brings a vast pressure to perform."

I jumped out of my chair. "Can someone around here speak English? I don't know what the freakin' hell is going on!"

Dad wrapped his arms around me. "Steroids, baby. Those pills in your bag are steroids."

"Those aren't my poison ivy pills," I mumbled.

Mom hugged me on the other side. "These are the steroids you hear about on the news. The kind that are illegal."

"Can you tell us where these pills came from?" Detective Carrod said.

I stared at the floor. The tile was scuffed. Yellow foam stuck out of a rip in the seat of my chair. The desk legs were gray metal. The air stunk of my game sweat and Mom's nerves.

Footsteps out in the locker room meant girls had been allowed in to get their stuff. I wanted to fling open the door and yell for them to get in here. Gonzo would be like, *Dude, this is totally bogus.* Bubble would tell them *Not Savvy, no. She's cool.* Even Lori might say—oh God, I pray she'd say—*Savvy may not always respect the rules, but she plays by them.*

"Mark, maybe we should get a lawyer," Mom whispered.

"I don't need a lawyer," I whispered. "Those pills aren't mine."

Detective Carrod smiled, sharp teeth aimed at my throat. "I'm sorry, Savvy. I didn't catch what you said."

"Can you hear me now?" I shouted. "Those are not my pills!"

"We're trying to understand why they were in your bag. Were you holding them for someone else?"

"No. That's stupid."

"Did you leave it out today?" Dad said. "Maybe in the gym or even in the locker room."

"I don't know. Maybe. I suppose I could have." I tossed my bag wherever I felt like it. During practice, I shoved it under the bleachers. After games, I dumped it in the hall while I went to the snack machines or concession table. The only reason the bag got locked up today was because the tournament people insisted on it. They didn't want iPods and money stolen—neither of which I had.

"She's careless, Detective," Mom said. "Someone must have seen her bag lying around and hid them in there."

"Why would someone do that?" Detective Carrod said.

"To frame me, that's why. You saw how dirty that team from Newport played. They could beat us up but they couldn't beat us. Plan B—get me in trouble so . . ." I croaked out the last few words. ". . . so I can't play in the elimination round tomorrow."

"Let me explain how this came about," Detective Carrod said. "Someone went into the locker room during your game, saw a couple of pills on the floor."

"Who?" Mom said.

The cop ignored her question, went on with her story. "This person looked through the holes in the lockers, trying to find out where the pills might have fallen from. So she could slip them back."

"What stupid fool would do that?" I said. The holes on the

locker-baskets were about the size of a pea—just wide enough so air could circulate through wet towels and sweaty socks. Only a total idiot would spend time peeking through those holes.

"She spotted the bag of pills. Coupled with hearing you admit to using steroids to one of your friends, she became concerned."

"Are you flippin' kidding me? I told Gonzo—Nina Gonzalez—that I had poison ivy." I pulled down my sock, showed the rash. "That's what the stupid idiot heard. Not me confessing I was taking drugs."

"Savvy is on prednisone," Dad said.

My face burned. "Daddy, I don't know anything about those pills. I swear."

"I know, honey. I know."

"Mark, we should just take her home," Mom said.

"Mrs. Christopher, that's not in anyone's best interest. Not until we finish our discussion." Detective Carrod turned back to me. "Mrs. Latham called the police. They quickly referred this matter to me. I've been investigating this problem for months now in this area."

"Are you even sure they're steroids?" my father asked. "They look like vitamins or extra-strength ibuprofen."

"Trust me, I've seen too much of this stuff. Our lab will test them to confirm, but I know this is Winstrol—street name *winnies*."

"Whatever they are, someone put them in my bag," I said. "I didn't."

"Savvy, those baskets are tight to prevent theft. There is no gap big enough to slip those pills into your basket, even if someone flattened the bag to a single layer. The only way to get those pills in there is to unlock your lock. Does anyone besides you have the combination to your lock?"

"I don't know," I said. "Let me think."

This was my chance to get this whole thing off my back. It would take a convincing lie. Like all kids, I could spin off everyday fibs: *Yeah, my homework's done* or *No, I don't like him* or *I did not use your shampoo.* To come up with something major, I needed a clear head.

Free throw line. Slow my breathing. Me and the ball.

Goggles had left the game at the same time I did. I could say she followed me to the locker room when I went to change my socks.

Eye on the basket. Feel the shot. I saw it as clearly as if it actually had happened.

Goggles sneaks in behind me.

Pretending to head for the bathroom, she stops and watches me open my combination lock. The whole time thinking—planning—*realizing*—she has a perfect way to getting me out of the tournament. Even half a minute is enough to open my locker and put the pills in.

On her way back to the bench, she gets her mother to call the cops.

Or maybe she gives her the combination and tells her to do the dirty work. A girl that nasty must have an equally wicked mother. She probably feeds steroids to Goggles with her dog chow.

Maybe it was someone else on Power. If they played dirty on the court, chances were they played dirty off it.

Maybe it was someone on another team. Maybe one of those nice girls from Lowell isn't feeling so chummy after we beat them.

Maybe one of my teammates did it. You know you're making a huge contribution to the team. You're finally making friends. But someone gets jealous when you take her starting position.

Maybe someone like Lori Penske did this to me.

"I'm gonna throw up," I said.

Dad pushed a wastebasket at me.

I vomited up the *maybes* until there was nothing left but spit.

CHAPTER TWENTY-SEVEN

Twenty minutes later we were still at it. Dad's face looked like an overripe tomato, Mom had shredded a whole packet of tissues, and I felt as helpless as Aunt Betty must have, all those weeks in the hospital.

Detective Carrod was like a pit bull with me in her jaws. "The only way we can help you—and kids like you—is to know who gave you the pills."

"How many times does she have to tell you they're not hers?" Mom asked.

"Not one more time," Dad said. "Unless you're going to arrest my daughter, we're out of here."

I was trying to muster strength back into my legs so I could stand up when Jennifer Kronos peeked in. "Excuse me. Detective Carrod, is it? I understand that there've been drugs found in the locker room."

"This is a private matter, Coach."

Kronos ignored her, looked directly at my parents. "I won't stand by and see what happened to me happen to Savvy."

Fitz crowded in behind her. "Ignore her. She has nothing to say worth listening to."

"The hell I don't!" Kronos snapped.

She crowded into the office with Fitz right behind, looking like his eyes would shoot blood. "You have no right to interfere with these people," he said.

"*Me* interfere? That's rich coming from you, Fitzgerald," Kronos said. "I thought you changed. But you're up to your old tricks."

Fitz looked straight at me, a strange pleading in his eyes. "Don't listen to her. She's was a liar back then and she's still lying."

Detective Carrod sat quietly, a little smile on her face as if she were watching television and not two adults going at it.

"Someone care to explain what's going on here?" Dad said.

Kronos squatted next to me and took my hands in hers. "When I played for Bill Fitzgerald in high school, he gave me amphetamines."

Fitz snorted his disgust. "Liar."

"Huh?" I said. That Twilight Zone haze settled in my brain, making me stupid.

"Senior year, one game away from playing in the state championship, I came down with mono. Thought I could tough it out, still play. But I dragged through warm-ups, told Fitz I was wiped. He said he had just the thing to perk me up. 'No-Doz,' he said."

Fitz dropped an F-bomb.

Detective Carrod tapped her pen against her teeth, her gaze shifting back and forth between the two coaches. For the moment, she had forgotten about me.

Kronos tightened her grip on my fingers. "Savvy, I popped a couple, and ten minutes later I had to be peeled off the ceiling, I was so out of control. My parents rushed me to the hospital. The tox screen showed amphetamines."

Mom put her hand to her mouth. "Is this true, Bill?"

"Of course not. After all these years, she's repeated the lie so much, I think she believes it," Fitz said. "Yeah, there was an incident, but I had absolutely nothing to do with it—other than become her fall guy. Kronos concocted the story to protect her college prospects. Cost me my high school coaching career."

"How? If it's not true," Dad said.

"Someone saw me hand her a couple of pills. They were salt tablets. But her so-called witness was just the little *oomph* she needed to make her fiction sound like fact."

Kronos stood, faced down Fitz. "And yet, here we are—another one of your star players being caught with drugs."

"They aren't my drugs," I mumbled.

"You pushing amps by the bag now, Bill?"

"They're steroids," Mom said.

"Terri, please," Dad said.

"Savvy wouldn't do this," Fitz said. "She doesn't need to."

Kronos squeezed Mom's shoulder. "Be glad, Terri. Glad you found out before it's too late."

"Please, God," I whispered. "Just get me out of here."

Dad took my elbow, hauled me out of the chair. "We're done."

"Go ahead," Detective Carrod said. "But I'll be in touch."

○=○=○=○=

Mrs. Latham caught up to us in the back hall. "I just spoke to the commissioner. I'm afraid . . ."

My stomach soured. "No. Please."

"She's still in discussion with the national office about whether or not to disqualify Fire. The SBA has a strict policy regarding performance-enhancing substances. At the very least, I'm afraid we can't let Savvy play until this is resolved. I'm sorry."

I raced for the door, stopped when I saw my teammates and their parents hanging out in the parking lot. "I can't go out there."

"I'll unlock the front door, let you out that way," Mrs. Latham said.

"I'll go get the car," Dad said.

"Wait. If you go to the car without me, they'll think I got arrested."

"What do you want us to do, Savvy?" Mom said.

"Let's just go. Like it's a normal day. Just go." I stepped outside. Beyond the glare of the lights, the night was dark and cold.

Gonzo ran to me and slipped her arm through mine. "Hey, dude."

My teammates circled around me.

"You okay?" Bubble grinned, trying to make it so.

"What happened?" Bailey asked. "Everyone's saying you got busted."

"They found pills in my bag. They're not mine. I don't know anything about them. Or how they got there. This whole thing sucks."

"They aren't yours?" Lori said.

"What did she just say?" Molly snapped.

"What do we do now?" Bubble said.

Gonzo opened her mouth but no words came out.

"Play like you know how." I waved them away and walked

alone to the car. Parents watched me, some faces clouded with confusion, others with doubt.

Eye on the basket.

A hundred feet to the car.

Don't rush.

Fifty feet to the car.

All you, Savvy. Like you can.

I got into the car, buckled in, and sat up straight. Dad drove out of the parking lot, a tiny muscle jumping in the back of his neck. Two vertebrae fused—does that hurt him?

When we were out of sight, I melted into the backseat and cried my fool heart out.

CHAPTER TWENTY-EIGHT

My one thing.

Basketball. As natural to me as breathing. As necessary to me as sunlight.

In the rare moments when I had dared to think about not playing, it was in terms of injury or illness. A blown knee. A busted-up back. A heart condition. Not pills in my gym bag.

Everyone knew steroids were for guys. Olympic track stars who wanted to run faster than anyone in the world. Major League Baseball players who wanted to break home-run records and make a hundred million dollars. High school football players—like Marc—who wanted to get big enough to interest college scouts.

Yet Detective Carrod didn't seem the least bit surprised that a girl might have a bag full of them.

Fitz was always on me to boost my game. It made sense that he could—*maybe*—give Jennifer Kronos a hit of speed back in the day to boost her game. Instead of winning the state championship, she got herself a trip to the hospital.

"Stop the car!" I yelled.

Dad pulled over to the side of the road and parked the car. "Are you all right, Savvy?"

"No. Yes, I mean. I will be. I need you to take me to the hospital. I want to get one of those drug tests. Like Ms. Kronos had."

"A tox screen?" Mom said.

"Yeah. When I come back clean, that'll prove those drugs aren't mine."

"Terri, why didn't we think of that?" Dad said. "We've got to do this."

My mother rubbed her forehead. "I don't see how we can call the doctor now. Not ten o'clock on a Sunday night. Especially not on the holiday weekend."

"Take me to the emergency room," I said.

"This isn't an emergency. They'll turn us away."

"Not if you tell them I went psycho or something. I can fake it." Fake it because I was only a heartbeat from going there.

Dad got out of the car, motioned me to join him. Mom peered through the windshield at us. I had no clue where we were. Heavy brush lined the road. The air chilled me. A wispy cloud passed in front of the moon.

"Once you get tested, there's no turning back," Dad said.

"Daddy, you don't believe me."

He smiled, a fat tearing trickling down his cheek. "I do."

"Then get me tested. Tonight."

He hugged me, his shoulder soaking up what was left of my tears.

○=○=○=○=

I nibbled my lip, trying to keep from crying. Funny how you can run out of energy or excitement but have an unlimited supply of tears.

"A week? But I need the test done like, tonight! I want to play tomorrow."

"This kind of a test is done by a specialty lab," Dr. Anna Chiamara said. "They won't even pick up your specimen until Monday. Dear me, I forgot. It's Columbus Day weekend. Their driver won't come until Tuesday. The results will be back about a week after that."

"I peed in the cup. What else do I have to do?"

"I'm ordering some blood work. Some our lab will do, some will have to go out."

"I thought a urine test was all I needed."

She smiled, showing a big gap between her two front teeth. "I want to do a liver panel and some endocrinology studies. Anabolic steroid use can cause havoc with a female system."

"I already told you—I don't do steroids."

Her gaze strayed to my biceps.

"I do farm work," I said.

"Hmm."

"Are you deaf like everyone else? Sheesh, I swear—"

"Savvy!" Dad's voice sounded like a whip from out in the hall.

"Your socks are bloody," Dr. Chiamara said.

"It's just poison ivy."

"Since you're here, let's get that cleaned up."

I stripped off my socks and sneakers. Dr. Chiamara dabbed my ankles with wet gauze. It felt good.

"So back to the steroid thing," she said.

"Here comes the"—I lowered my voice to a whisper—"*I'll pretend I'm the kid's friend* lecture."

"No. Here comes the *If you want me to send out your blood*

tests, you'll darn well listen lecture. Otherwise, you can call your family doctor on Tuesday."

I hadn't eaten in eight hours, I was tired, I was scared, and this frizzy-haired doctor wanted me to sit still for a DARE lecture. "You got me by the ankles. Lecture away."

Dr. Chiamara laughed. "Do you know how anabolics work, Savannah?"

"They make muscles bigger."

"Why?" she said.

"I don't know. They make you more manly, I guess."

"Good way to put it. Anabolic steroids are synthetic derivatives of testosterone, the male hormone. Athletes and bodybuilders take steroids to increase muscle mass and strength."

Dr. Chiamara rinsed my ankles with a bottle of sterile water. It was so soothing that I felt guilty about being rude. But if I lost my attitude, I'd have nothing to hold on to.

"The use of anabolics among young people is still increasing. The consequences are dire. Cancer. Liver damage. Injury to tendons and ligaments. Blood disorders. Depression. High blood pressure."

"That's guys," I said. "Girls don't do that. Okay, maybe some of those weight lifters. They slap on breast implants and call themselves women, but they're so juiced up, who knows what they are. Real female athletes don't get into that."

"You kidding? Female athletes have used anabolics for over thirty years. In the seventies, Communist-bloc countries pumped up their female sprinters and shot putters to give them a boost in the Olympics. The practice spread to U.S. sprinters and other track athletes. Team sports, perhaps.

And there's a very small but scary trend of girls who want to sculpt their bodies to look better in a bikini."

"That's just sick."

She stuffed my socks and sneakers into a plastic bag and handed me a pair of hospital booties. "In addition to all the other dangers, a woman using steroids may develop male characteristics. And if we're talking long-term use in girls who are still developing, some of these male characteristics may be irreversible."

I jumped off the table. "Are we done yet?"

"I'll have the lab come draw your blood."

"Fine. Whatever. Stick a hundred needles in me. Just no more lectures."

Dr. Chiamara slipped her stethoscope into her pocket. On her way out the door, she turned for one last word. "Savannah. Another consequence of steroid abuse?"

"What?"

"'Roid rage."

"Don't tempt me," I whispered. "Don't friggin' tempt me."

CHAPTER TWENTY-NINE

I sniffled and moaned and raged and couldn't get to sleep. I had just checked my cell phone, expecting a bunch of messages. There were only two. Gonzo texted to tell me she'd call me tomorrow, after the games. Bubble called to say, "Hang in there, Savvy."

Neither one said: "We know you didn't do it."

Callie climbed into bed with me and snuggled like we were little girls. "Wanna talk about it?"

"No."

"What do you think happened?"

"How the hell should I know? Someone framed me, obviously."

"Did you tell the cops that?" Callie said. "That someone at the tournament is out to get you?"

"I told you I don't want to talk about it."

"I'm just trying to make sure you're all right." She shook my shoulder. "Want to shoot some baskets? I'll go out with you. Maybe I'll even put a couple up."

My laugh sounded like a strangled rooster. "You'll go out in the middle of the night with the coyotes and slugs and bats. Right."

"If it'll help."

"Did Mom and Dad put you up to this?" I asked.

"This what?"

"Being . . . nice to me."

Callie stiffened. "I don't need anyone to tell me what to do."

"Sorry. I'm just . . ."

"Wiped. I know." She snuggled back against me.

"Cal, what if I never get to play ever again?" The sobbing started, ripping the back of my throat.

"You'll play."

"What if I don't?"

"You will. You have to." She rolled over so her back was to me and didn't say another word.

I lay there, gulping tears and staring up at the underside of the top bunk. Maybe I'm really asleep, I thought. Maybe I'll wake up and we'll be back in New Mexico and Dad would never have fallen off the roof and Callie would be normal and Mom would be chilled out.

And maybe not.

O═O═O═O═

At breakfast, everyone except Aunt Betty looked like the dawn-of-the-living-dead.

"They aren't Savvy's pills," Callie said.

Dad buttered his toast so hard that the bread broke with a pop. The whole family was on a knife's edge. Aunt Betty sipped her tea, watched the discussion. She was the only one in my family who met my eye without some sort of cringe or confused blink.

"Can you shed light on these pills, Callie?" he said.

"Of course not. Why would I be able to? I just know they aren't Savvy's."

"She could be in a lot of trouble," Mom said. "If you know something, please tell us."

"Savvy's an idiot, but she wouldn't do something this stupid. I swear, she can't be guilty of something like this. I know it in my gut."

"We do too," Mom said.

"We have to give the police something more than our gut feelings," Dad said.

The sugar in the orange juice finally cleared the fuzz in my brain. "Those pills must be Marc's."

"Shut up!" Callie stood up so fast, her chair tipped over. "How could you even think that?"

"You shut up. Who else could it be?"

"I was up all night with you. And you pay me back by accusing Marc?"

"All he talks about is getting big enough to get a D-1 scholarship."

"Savvy, let's not get ahead of oursel—" Mom stopped when Dad clutched her hand.

"Callie, have you allowed Marc in your bedroom?" he said.

The veins in my sister's neck bulged. "I know the rules."

I snorted. "I caught him in there. I never told, but he's been up there a couple of times."

"Calliope." Mom sounded genuinely shocked. "What were you thinking?"

"Are you freakin' kidding me?" I said. "Come on, Mom. Get your head out of your—out of the sand."

"We weren't doing anything wrong." Callie's voice had a

sandpaper edge to it. "And furthermore . . . those pills certainly weren't his."

I leaned across the table, got in her face. "Oh yeah? Maybe we oughtta ask the golden boy about that."

"You leave him out of this!"

"No. I want to hear what Marc has to say for himself."

"Say about what?" Marc stood in the back door. "Sorry, I knocked but no one answered. What's up?"

"Nothing. We are so out of here." Callie stood.

I grabbed her around the waist. "Not until I ask him."

"What are you doing? Let me go."

"Savannah," Mom said. "Let your sister go."

Callie bit my arm. It hurt like hell but no way was I letting her go. "Not until I ask Marc."

"Hey, hey," Marc said, "I'll answer whatever, but let her go. What're you, nuts?"

"No! Marc, go home. This is a family matter," Callie cried. "I'll call you later."

"Whatever." He gave us an odd look and turned to leave.

"Wait," Dad said. "We need to talk, Marc."

Callie kicked at me but I wouldn't let go. I'd choke her until her stupid boyfriend told the truth.

Mom slipped her arms in between us to pry us apart. "Enough. Sit. Both of you."

"You too, Marc," Dad said.

I let Callie go. Neither of us moved, waiting for the other one to sit first.

"You were all told to sit," Aunt Betty said in her teacher's voice.

I slumped into my chair.

"Will someone tell me what's going on?" Marc had remained standing.

"Please, Marc. Just go home," Callie sobbed.

Give the kid credit for manning up—he ignored her and stared straight at my father. "What's this about, Mr. Christopher?"

Dark circles ringed my father's eyes. Pain, I realized. Sitting on a bleacher all day followed up by *Savvy almost goes to jail* had strained his back and neck. He'd be miserable for weeks.

"Daddy, please," Callie whispered. "Please, if you love me, just leave him out of this."

That was her life's theme, I realized. If you love me, just leave me out of anything bad or sad or scary or ugly.

My father put his hand over hers, gave a little squeeze. He had done the same thing for me last night when Detective Carrod was asking me questions. Callie pulled away and ran out of the room. Apparently the gesture hadn't comforted her any more than it had me.

Dad stood so he could face Marc. "Let's go outside."

They went out to the back porch and, a minute later, I heard Marc explode an F-bomb.

CHAPTER THIRTY

No one had clued the world that it had crashed down on me.

Days like this were why people loved New England. The trees blazed with color. A warm wind ruffled the grass in the low pasture. On the crest of the hill, the sheep were the only clouds in the endless sky.

Marc's parents had called mine and asked them to go over there to talk. Callie told me she hated me, hoped I would die, and had Alyssa come get her.

Alyssa came over to the barn to talk to me. I was there because I didn't want to be inside, didn't have the energy to hike up to the high pasture, and couldn't bear to even look at my basketball court.

She hugged me. "It's going to be okay."

"Does everyone in the whole world know?" My stomach heaved at the notion.

"Callie told me because she was worried about you."

"Yeah, right."

"She just isn't good at expressing herself."

"That's because she's a selfish bitch."

Alyssa gave me another hug, didn't let go this time. "You took a blood test, right? It'll clear you and everyone will forget the whole thing."

I shook my head. "How can I go to school tomorrow?"

"Hold your head up high—and hold on until the blood test comes back. Be strong, and everyone will know you didn't do this."

"Damn right. Marc did."

Alyssa smoothed my hair. "Don't go throwing accusations around, sweetie. It'll cause more trouble than good. Just hold tight, it'll clear up soon. Okay?"

"Don't you get it? The championship round of the national qualifier is today and they won't let me play."

"You have another one next month, right?"

"How do you know?"

"Your sister told me. She cares about you, really. Just keep calm, Savvy. It'll all be over really soon."

They drove off, leaving me wondering why Alyssa couldn't be my big sister instead of Callie.

○▪○▪○▪○▪

Gonzo got dropped off around lunchtime.

"Oh no! Is Fire out of it already?" I asked.

"One and done, baby. Hey, got any food? I didn't feel like eating after the game." She went to the kitchen and made a peanut butter and jelly sandwich. "Want one?"

"No. Thanks."

"Where is everyone?"

"Callie went somewhere with Alyssa."

"What about the 'rents?"

"Don't ask." I had promised my parents I wouldn't repeat the accusations I made about Marc. They'd been gone over two hours now.

"Betty?"

"Mr. Otis took her to see one of their friends in a nursing home."

"Stinks when all your friends are old, huh? She's lucky to have her boy-toy Georgie." Gonzo waited for me to laugh.

I was in no mood. "So how bad was it? Tell me it wasn't Power who knocked us out."

"That team from Woonsocket. They're good but not so good we shouldn't have beat them. We were just off our game." Gonzo took a big bite, washed it down with milk. "The good news is, after we lost, some of us stayed to watch Power in their first game. They got smoked."

"Ah. Sweet deal."

"They took an early lead but when other team started to catch up, Power went into dirtbag mode. And because they had good refs officiating—yippee for that—Goggles fouled out before the half. Without her clogging the middle of the court, the other team wore them down. Won by six points."

"Justice is a lovely thing," I said, giving her the perfect opening to tell me she knew I was totally innocent.

But all she said was, "Let's go toss some hoops."

"I don't feel like it."

"Don't go all weird over this. You're only fourteen. They'll just send you to some program or something. You do the twelve steps, everyone gets off your back. You play, we win. End of story."

An icy shiver ran through me. "You don't believe me."

"Of course I do."

The split second pause before she said that told me she had doubts.

"Know what? I'm kinda tired," I said. "Up half the night and all that. Could you call your mom to come get you? I have to go take a nap."

She went to tap my fist but I wouldn't offer it, so she tapped my forehead instead. "Hey, dude. Go ahead. Patriots are on, playing the Colts. I'll watch until you're ready to hang out."

Loyalty wasn't gonna cut it. I needed absolute faith in my innocence from my best friend. Not that I could tell her that. Gonzo would swear she believed me, all the time pretending not to have that wiggle in her mind that said *Do I really, really know this girl?*

"That's all right," I said. "Go ahead home."

"My mother can't pick me up. She's food shopping, my father's fishing and . . . well, we all know I can't ask one of my sibs. I'll just hang here. Maybe you'll feel better in a while."

"Take my bike. Ride home."

"Yo. You throwin' me out, dude?"

"I just want to be alone," I said.

"And I want you not to be alone."

"Fine. You stay. I'll leave." Before Gonzo could react, I dashed out the back door. Running at top speed, I passed the barn and hurdled the fence. I leaped over the boulders and rises of the low pasture, my heart pounding, before I took the next fence at a dead run.

Gonzo couldn't keep up, not with short legs and an eye out for sheep dung. I didn't care what I stepped on or in. A gopher hole and broken ankle might be a mercy today.

I crossed the dirt road, jumped the next fence, and

started climbing. I was slowed by the murderous slope of the hill, and my skin burned even though my stomach was like ice.

Gonzo jogged up the road. It was twice as long but half as likely to explode one's heart. Okay, so she cared enough to chase me. Didn't mean I had to let her catch me.

Cutting through the birches, I scrambled over the stone wall that the settlers had built three hundred years ago. It took great strength to move these rocks without a backhoe or tractor. Our Christopher ancestors were mighty strong people.

No one accused *them* of taking steroids.

I stumbled in the woods, searching for one of the main trails. A branch scratched my cheek and thorns ripped at me. I swore, pushed sideways through some scrub pines—and tripped over a mess so bloody that only the plastic yellow tag told me what it was.

One of our lambs.

"Oh God," I howled, and ran back to the high pasture.

Manny had already come out of the shade, drawn by my cries. I grabbed his collar. "You stupid mutt. You're supposed to take care of them. What is wrong with you, what is wrong—"

Gonzo yanked my arm. "Stop it! You're yelling at a dog, for Pete's sake."

"He's supposed to know. Four thousand years of breeding, two months of training, and he's just sitting here like nothing happened?"

Manny tore out of my grasp and circled the sheep, his ears

flattened and his stare cold. Even he thought I was the bad guy. "You dumb stupid mutt."

"Stop it, Savvy. He's still a puppy. Don't be mad at him."

I sat in the grass with my face pressed to my knees. Gonzo sat down next to me. "What's wrong?"

"I found a dead—" I waved at the woods.

"I'm sorry, dude. Honest. This sucks."

I looked at her—*really looked.* Justice had been delivered in one thing, at least. I burst out laughing, kept at it like a madman. Rolling in the grass, kicking my feet.

Gonzo shook my shoulder, tried to make me stop. "Savvy, maybe I should call your mother."

I gasped for air. "And tell her what?"

"That . . . um . . . you are a little . . . um . . . unsettled."

"It's you who is about to be unsettled." I sat up, and pointed to where she was sitting.

Gonzo jumped up, cursing at the mess on the back of her jeans. I followed her back down to the house, roaring with laughter.

If sheep poop was the only justice I was going to get today, I'd take it.

CHAPTER THIRTY-ONE

Just when I thought things couldn't get worse, they did.

"Marc's parents are taking him over to the hospital to have a blood test. They're anxious to allay any suspicions people might have." Dad cleared his throat. "Because of his association with this . . . discovery."

"They're talking about suing us for slander," Callie said. "Why couldn't you keep quiet? He hates me. And I hate you, Savvy. Forever."

Marc's parents made him break it off with Callie. She tried to sleep in the living room but Dad wouldn't allow it. She took to sleeping in the hall, rather than share a room with me. Her silence was as impenetrable as a bank vault. All she did was huddle in a blanket and have whispered conversations on her cell phone with Alyssa.

The next day, I begged to stay home from school.

"You don't go, you'll look guilty," Dad said.

"Besides, unless Nina tells what happened, no one will even know," Mom said.

Right. Maybe in my mother's la-la land, but in Taylor Middle School, bad news travels fast. The nightmare began the minute I got on the bus. I missed the good old days when I was merely a giraffe. Now I was a juicer chick with all the garbage that went with that rep. My only hope was that some kid from the school would get kidnapped or murdered. A shameful thing to think, even for a second, but that's how low I had sunk.

Gonzo made small talk at lunch. Leah and Jamie chatted around me, not exactly excluding me, but clearly they wished I would sit somewhere else. Amazingly, Alyssa's sister Maddie came over to the table and squeezed in between me and Gonzo. "My sister told me what happened. How're you doing?"

"Yeah, you know. Pretty sucky."

"Just get through the next few days—you'll be okay. Hey, I made you some brownies. So you'd know I'm thinking of you." Maddie pulled a plasticware container out of her bag.

"Wow. Thanks. Let me wrap these up so you can have the container back."

"Nah. Just bring it over later this week."

"Sure. Okay."

She squeezed my shoulder as she got up. "I gotta go to chorus. Hang in."

"Thanks." I popped open the container, breathed in deep chocolate that normally would send me into ecstasy. Even fudge brownies wouldn't settle my stomach.

"Yo, dude. What's up with that?" Gonzo said.

Jamie and Leah stopped their too-loud, too-cheerful conversation and listened.

I shrugged. "Alyssa probably put her up to it."

"Why?"

I glared at her. "She believes me when I say I'm innocent."

"I was just asking. You gonna share the loot?" Gonzo said.

"Yeah, Savvy. How 'bout it," Jamie said.

Leah came around the table, slid next to me and grabbed the container. "Thanks, pal."

Thank Alyssa. Why couldn't my sister show the same consideration? Callie carried her wounded silence around like a club.

The thaw in my gut lasted only until world history. I got in early and pushed my seat as far forward as it would go without people noticing. I wanted to get out of taunting range of Fish Face and Buzz Cut, whose real names were Derek and Xander.

Mrs. Potter talked for about twenty minutes about mad cow disease in Canada. That brought to mind the snippet of conversation Mr. Otis and Aunt Betty had about antibiotics and livestock. If this had been a normal day, I might have asked Mrs. Potter about it. Instead, I slumped in my chair and tried to look like I was a five-foot tall nobody instead of an accused criminal.

Mrs. Potter passed out a worksheet and left us for a minute. Going to get her afternoon Diet Coke, I knew.

Thirty seconds later, Fish Face and Buzz Cut started in. When Buzz Cut whispered, "You grow balls yet, Christopher?" I decided to unload a little 'roid rage on the jerk.

I got up and shoved his desk—with him in it—all the way to the back of the room.

The fear in his face was better than any pan of brownies. "You happy?" I said.

"Huh?" His gaze went to the door, probably praying Mrs. Potter would come in to save him. Everyone watching probably hoped she wouldn't.

"All those notes and whispers and poking me in the back." Leaning so close that I could smell pizza on his breath, I pressed my hands over his. "All that attention could only mean one thing."

"Wh-wh-what?" He hunched his shoulders as if I was going to clobber him.

I turned and faced the class. "Isn't it obvious? Poor kid's got the hots for me but he's too shy to say it."

"That's wack," he sputtered.

I mustered up confidence by pretending I was Gonzo, the drama queen. "I'm afraid I have bad news for you. No matter how hard you try, Xander—I can't go out with you."

Fish Face giggled like a girl. Relieved, I think, that I went after Buzz Cut and not him.

"You're crazy."

"Because—" I scanned the classroom, my stomach twisted in a giant knot but *all me, the ball, the basket*. "Because Xander, you're just too short for me."

The class exploded with laughter. Before I even got back to my desk, kids were ragging on him.

Score one for the good guys, I thought.

⚬≡⚬≡⚬≡⚬≡

After school, I was surprised to find my mother at home. I'd seen enough cop shows to know the blue sedan next to her car was an unmarked cruiser. Would some news copter swoop down over the trees to broadcast the scene as my butt got hauled off to jail?

Detective Carrod was in the living room, drinking coffee with Mom and Aunt Betty. "Hello, Savannah," she said.

"Savvy, sit," Mom said.

"I'm afraid that we have indeed confirmed that the pills in your bag are *winnies*."

"Winstrol," Mom said. Overnight she'd become an expert in steroid abuse.

Detective Carrod glanced at her, then continued. "We have no interest in charging you with possession. We want to nail the scum selling these substances to young people. If you can help us, you'd be doing yourself and other young people in this community a big service."

I clenched my hands and swallowed my fury. "I already told you all I know. Which is nothing."

"Did your coach give you those pills?" she said.

"No."

"You can clear Mr. Fitzgerald of suspicion if you can share anything you know about where they came from."

"They aren't my pills. I don't know how they got in my bag. End of story." I stood, grabbed my backpack, and went to my room.

I stretched out on my bunk, not at all surprised when Mom came in a few minutes later. I rolled over, my face to the wall. See how she liked me playing the Callie routine.

Mom smoothed my hair. I was too tired to slap her hand away. "Fitz didn't give you those pills?" she whispered.

I rolled over so I could meet her gaze. "No."

"You don't know how they got in your bag?"

"No."

She pulled me into her arms. "I will choose to believe you, then."

I pushed back. "You don't have to work this hard to believe Callie."

Mom looked away.

"She sneezes and you're there to blow her nose for her. *Don't get upset, honey. Mommy and Daddy caught your snots for you.*"

"Savvy, please."

"It's the truth."

"I'm sorry," she whispered.

"I don't want an apology. I just want to know why."

My mother buried her face in her hands. "She's not strong enough to carry around all this fear by herself."

I got up and instinctively grabbed my basketball from the closet. I dropped it like it was on fire. Its *pum* on the hard floor sounded like a gunshot. Screw this, I thought, and snatched it before it could bounce again.

"You know what, Mom?"

She looked up at me, her face splotchy with tears.

"I got these muscles by lifting heavy things," I said. "Maybe if you let Callie do her own heavy lifting once in a while, she'd get strong too."

"Maybe," she whispered.

I went out to shoot some hoops.

CHAPTER THIRTY-TWO

Seven more days of freakin' hell. No other way to describe it.

Gonzo, Jamie, Leah, and a couple of others went out of their way to pal around with me, but the obvious effort it took them was more irksome than being shunned. One sixth-grade boy named Richie dogged me, convinced I could score him some pot. Buzz Cut got me called down to the office because he told Mrs. Potter that I had threatened to rip his head off.

I showed the principal a couple of Buzz Cut's and Fish Face's notes. That got them a week's detention and me transferred into the same class as Maddie Bouchard. She greeted me warmly but didn't introduce me to her friends. Apparently all contact was on her terms.

Bubble called me every evening, trying to cheer me up. On Thursday she said, "Hey, Mrs. Penske had us doing the dumbest drills this afternoon."

"Mrs. Penske?" I said.

"Oh. No one told you?"

"Told me what?"

"Fitz has been suspended from coaching. Until . . . you know."

Yeah, I knew all right.

I called Lori up. "Did you snitch on me?"

"Who is this?"

"Like you don't have caller ID?"

She exhaled noisily. "I didn't snitch to the police about you."

"No? Who had the most to gain?" I yelled.

"You apparently," she said, and snapped her phone off.

On Friday, Aunt Betty came down with the flu from a flu shot. She escaped hospitalization by a whisper and lots of chicken soup that Dad made for her.

Molly called to ask if she could come over Saturday morning before basketball.

"I appreciate the offer," I said. "But you won't cheer me up."

"I know. You promised to show me your dog."

I walked her out to the low pasture. The sheep lowed when they saw me, thinking I'd brought them some hay. Manny kept them in line until I called for them. Then he stepped aside and let them crowd the fence.

"He won't come," Molly said.

"No. Not unless I call him specifically."

"But Anatolians are friendly. That's what the books say."

"Are you going to get one?" I asked.

"I've been saving money since my German shepherd died. That was two years ago."

"Sorry. You didn't want another dog right away?"

"I don't rush into things until I do my research. You should know that by now, Savvy."

I leashed up Manny and walked with Molly around the whole farm. A wind had come up, spinning dry leaves around us.

"You know what a sheepfold is, don't you?" Molly asked.

"Like a pen," I said. "My father and I talked about building one. Then we got Manny."

Molly bent to pat him, remembered not to before I had to warn her. "I read that in olden times they'd put sheep or goats in pens at night. And then the shepherd slept stretched across the gate so wolves or bears or even lions couldn't get in. Imagine that?"

"I don't think shepherds do that anymore." I shivered at the thought of putting myself between the sheep and a lion.

"They ride around in pickup trucks or on ATVs. At least, that's what I read." Molly's cell phone beeped. "It's my mom. She's down at your house. Time to go to my next appointment."

"Huh?"

"We're driving across town to see a Rhodesian Ridgeback."

"Oh. Sounds like fun." I walked her down to the driveway, and said, "Thanks for stopping by."

"Savvy—I researched the blood tests Gonzo said you had. You'll be cleared in a few days."

I scratched my nose. "That's if I didn't do what everyone thinks I did."

Molly hugged the life out of me. "I don't need any research to tell me that you didn't."

Later that night, Gonzo came over with a trophy for me. Fire had won that tournament without me. I tossed it in the trash.

○=○=○=○=

Saturday night I opened the door to Jennifer Kronos. I didn't invite her in, wasn't sure I should. "What're you doing here?"

"Your parents are expecting me."

I left her standing on the porch while I yelled for my

parents. I disappeared upstairs, sat at the computer while ignoring the block of stone formerly known as my sister on the top bunk. Mom had had to force her to go to school the day after Marc dumped her, but judging by the car full of girls who dropped her off after cheering, she was as popular as ever.

Nothing like accusations and a breakup to have your friends falling all over you to comfort you.

Five minutes later, Mom came upstairs. "Coach Kronos wants to talk to you."

"I have nothing to say to her."

"It's about this thing with Fitz."

Whoa. That was probably the one thing—other than Goggles being hauled off to a maximum security prison—that could entice me to talk to that woman.

Kronos sat outside, on the front steps. I was in no mood to be friendly, so I stood. "You have something to say?" I said.

"I wanted to chat about that episode I had with Fitz in high school."

"He didn't give me those pills," I said automatically. "Those aren't my pills."

She smiled, showing tiny lines around her eyes. "I'm the one confessing here."

I sat next to her. "I'll be the judge of that."

She dragged her fingers through her hair. "Fitz was right in one aspect. I've told the same story for so long, I've come to believe it myself. But he did the same thing."

I pressed my face into my knees and covered my head with my arms.

"Let me tell you what the truth is. I haven't admitted it to anyone in all these years. Savvy, please . . ."

I peeked out from under my arm. She slid down two steps so we could be eye to eye. "The truth is, Fitz did give me a couple tabs of speed. Well, maybe a better term than 'give' is that he *provided* me the stuff."

I jumped up. "What the hell? You said you were going to tell me the truth."

"I am. Let me finish. Please."

"Fine. Finish."

"I had had mono, was desperate to play. This was the state championship, Savvy. You can imagine how insane I was to be in the game."

"I suppose."

"I begged him all week leading up to the game. 'I just need a little boost, Coach. You gotta get me something.' We tried No-Doz but it wasn't enough. In practice, my legs felt like I was walking in sand. I begged him to get me something stronger. He had connections with a couple of college programs. Back in the eighties, greenies—amphetamines—were everywhere."

Without thinking, I picked up my basketball and shot at the basket. I missed but she pulled off an incredible rebound, tossed it to me.

"So how does this help me?" I shot again, made a rim-spinner.

Kronos shot from the free throw line, with such grace that I wanted to cry.

"Is Fitz pressuring you to . . ."

"No. Absolutely not."

"Are you sure?"

"Are you deaf?" I said.

Without even meaning to, we slipped into one on one. She moved the ball beautifully, like a six-foot-tall Gonzo. But she couldn't fly, not like I could. She had to take all her shots from farther out.

"I just want to make sure you're okay."

"Oh yeah, my life is just fantastic."

Kronos stopped mid-shot, let the ball trickle out of her hands. "Fitz refused to give me anything directly. He said we'd be better off just losing."

"So what happened?"

"It wasn't like I was trying to make myself something I wasn't. I was just trying to get back to where I was. And Fitz . . . well, he hated losing as much as I do. Still does.

"He let slip that he had taken some speed tabs off some bozo cross-country runner and had them in his desk. Said he hadn't gotten around to turning them in to the office or flushing them. Before the game, he asked me to go into his office, get him his water bottle. In the four years I had played for him, I never ran an errand for him. Never, ever.

"The desk was unlocked. Guy was paranoid—he always locked his desk. But it was unlocked, with the top drawer open. Inside that drawer was a half-open envelope. I didn't even have to pick it up to see the pills inside."

Kronos wiped her forehead. "I took two, had a bad reaction, and the rest is as we said."

"Except for the lies," I said.

"Yeah. His half-truth and my half-truth add up to one twenty-year-old lie."

"Why are you telling me this?"

"Because I don't want Fitz leaving his desk drawer unlocked for you."

"You sound like a freakin' made-for-TV movie. Sheesh."

"Coaches want to win, but even more, we get a kick out of seeing our stars shine. Savvy, you are so much like I was—the talent, the drive, the bright future. I just want to make sure—"

"Stop. Right there, you just shut up. I am so not you. And I hope to hell I never am."

I heaved the basketball into the woods and went back into the house.

O═O═O═O═

A full ten days after I got bounced from basketball, Dr. Chiamara showed up at our door.

"It's good news," she said. "Can I come in?"

The whole family gathered around the kitchen table, except for Callie. When she did speak, it was only to tell Mom or Dad that we were dead to her. They had carted her off to see a therapist. That was a royal waste of time because she wouldn't talk to the shrink. She had plenty to say to her friends, though.

Dr. Chiamara spread some papers across the table. "These are photocopies of Savannah's test results. I knew you'd want them. The first one is the urine test for Winstrol. Negative."

I jumped out of my seat. "Yes! I told you I didn't take those pills."

"Not so fast. Oral stanozolol—Winstrol—clears the body in two or three days, as opposed to the injectable, which can take weeks or even months. I had to battle your insurance company to get them to pay for a more sophisticated test."

She shuffled the papers, showed us another one. "This one tests the metabolites of stanozolol in the blood that linger for some time after the drug is stopped. This test was also negative."

Dad exhaled loudly, leaned back in his chair. "Thank God. And thank you, Dr. Chiamara, for all this."

"I told you," I said. "I told you and you didn't believe me."

Mom tilted her head, looked at me sideways. "Savvy, we said we did believe you."

"Your words, maybe. But I heard it in your voice, trust me. And now you know." I sat down hard, my moment of justice more bitter than sweet.

Dad kissed the top of my head and whispered, "I'm sorry."

Dr. Chiamara blushed and rustled her papers. "I also ordered an endocrine panel. Savannah is a perfectly normal female. No rise in testosterone, which we might have seen had she been taking anabolics for any length of time. All other indicators are in normal ranges."

"Now what?" I said. "How do I get back on the team?"

"If your parents give me permission, I could call the detective on the case and your basketball commissioner. Report these results to them."

"Yes! Yes! Please," I said.

"Absolutely," Dad said.

"I'll need you to sign these releases, giving me permission," Dr. Chiamara said.

"Do it," I said. "Like, right now."

My parents read the release forms. Aunt Betty got up and went to the refrigerator. A minute later, she set a huge ham sandwich in front of me. My stomach had been a train wreck for the past ten days. Suddenly it screamed for food. "How did you know I was hungry?"

Aunt Betty smiled. "I know you, Savannah."

That she did. Now everyone else would too.

NOVEMBER

CHAPTER THIRTY-THREE

The New Bedford qualifier was the last chance of the season for the Kent County Fire. This Veteran's Day weekend, I prayed we'd go all the way and not just to score a bid for Orlando.

Starved for competition, I was desperate to play as many games as possible—anywhere, anytime.

Mom's company had a convention in New York City over the weekend. Originally my father was supposed to go with her, and enjoy a paid mini-vacation. As the time neared, they crept around the house, whispering to each other.

"Maybe I'll stay home, take in some basketball," Dad said.

"Oh no," I said. "You go. I'll be fine."

Like I needed someone to hold my hand as I made my return to the court? I did, but admitting it made me too much like Callie. When she heard Dad say he couldn't leave us because she was *unstable,* she freaked. "Savvy and I are talking now. Right?"

Wrong. But I said, "Sure." My parents had baggy eyes and slumped shoulders. They really, really needed a break, even if it meant pretending Callie and I were cool—instead of ice-age cold—with each other.

As my parents packed the car on Thursday night, they kissed and hugged like teenagers. Good for them but *ugh* for us. Save the kissy-face for room service, not for your kids.

Aunt Betty got her cast off just in time to drive me to the tournament. Ava's mom and Bailey's father recognized her. She had taught them English in high school twenty years ago.

The steroid shadow still loomed over Fire. Once I tested clean, the SBA reinstated Fitz as coach. He only spoke to me in a group. No more one on ones to tell me how to boost my game. It was better that way—I couldn't shake the image of him leaving his desk unlocked.

Bubble hugged me all the time, like you'd do with someone who had survived a plane crash or cancer.

All of us left our gym bags with our families. Never again would we trust a locker room.

Lori avoided me like I was the disease of the week. I assumed she was hacked off because my return to the team bounced her out of center again.

Parents were too friendly to be anything but faking it. Didn't matter what my blood tests showed. The question of where the pills came from had never been answered. When Marc tested perfectly clean, his parents sent mine a bill for two hundred and twenty dollars to cover the cost of the blood test.

Gonzo and I pretended nothing had ever happened. She knew I knew that she had—in a tiny corner of her gut— doubted me. That unspoken *knowing* smoldered between us.

During the warm-ups of our Friday night game, I soaked in the game in all its glory. The leather in my hands. The hollow thum-thum of dribbling. The odor of bodies—shampoo and deodorant now, but when the game got going, we'd stink like struggle.

The horn sounded and our game against the Littleton Lions began. On our first possession, Molly bounced a pass to me in the paint. I hit a layup with my left hand, barely ruffling the net. Three seconds—and I was back, baby.

Our families and friends cheered like crazy, but the sweetest sound was *clunk clunk clunk* as Aunt Betty pounded her cane on the bleachers.

O═O═O═O═

We won that game easily and survived two tough games the next day. By the time we got to our third game Saturday evening, my legs felt like straw. That we were undefeated didn't matter. In a tournament this big, only the top team in each bracket would go on to play in Sunday's elimination round.

Every game was win or walk.

Playing in a different bracket, the Newport Power had crushed all their opponents and were already slated for the elimination round. Before getting another shot at Goggles, we had to get past the North Middlesex Ice.

The Ice had trounced the teams we had barely beaten. I understood why. We aimed to intimidate in warm-ups but they pulled it off, shooting around with a crispness that fit their team's name.

Fitz started us in zone defense, wanting to get a long look at what Ice would bring. Their center—a Maya Moore look-alike—got in the high post and pushed back at me to get some shooting room. I stood my ground and when she whirled to shoot, she knocked into me.

Tweet! "Charge," the ref called.

Gonzo inbounded to Molly and she found me in my favorite corner. I drained the shot and, like that, it was Fire 3, Ice zip.

We battled for every possession. Apart from the rare instances I could sneak into the corner, I had trouble getting shots off. Ice double-teamed me when I was outside. When I got in the paint, the Maya girl took me on alone.

In the middle of the first half, Fitz called time and subbed Lori in for Ava. "We need to cushion our score," he said. "Penske, I want you screening for Christopher so she can get more shots off. Christopher, you're forward on offense but then hustle back and play the lane on defense."

Lori blinked, said nothing. On the way out, I said to her, "If you get open, I'll find you," I said.

"Like I want the crumbs off your table?" she said. "Don't bother."

Ice pressed us full court on defense, trying to disrupt our rhythm. On offense, Maya slipped in and out of the paint like a shadow. On defense, she became an amoeba, clinging to me like a second skin.

With three minutes left in the half, Fitz called another time-out to give us a breather. Sweat plastered Bubble's curls flat on her forehead and Bailey's face looked like a red plum. The back of my shirt was soaked through.

I hadn't been this happy in weeks.

Molly poked me, pointed. Goggles stood near the door, with String Bean and another girl from Power. "What're they doing here?" she said.

"Free country," I mumbled. "Even maggots have the right of assembly."

When the game resumed, Bubble inbounded to Gonzo. The two of them dribbled the perimeter, playing keep-away until I could get open. I was rising for a shot when an Ice player reached over my shoulder.

Foul on her, free throw for me. I lined up, spinning the ball in my hands. Finding my focus. *Me and the ball. Me and the basket.*

A strange cheer leaked into my consciousness. Some kind of rhythmic nonsense, like the cheers we used to do in 10U.

Bailey caught my eye, shifted her glance to the door. Goggles and her teammates chanted in low tones. Even the official standing near me hadn't realized what they were saying. Girls blabbered all the time. Referees and coaches learned to shut it out.

I spun the ball again, trying to find that zone where it was all about what my body knew and not what my ears heard.

Gonzo called out, "All you, Savvy." Ice players reminded each other to rebound and their fans called "Dee-fense." Loud, familiar echoes, but all I heard was that low refrain coming from the corner. Nonsense unless you were me and knew what they were chanting—and why.

BAL-CO-ho.

Anyone who had followed sports in the past few years knew all about BALCO and the steroid scandal in professional sports. Don't, I told myself, but my gaze went to them like a fly on dog poop. Goggles grinned and wiggled her finger at me. Anyone watching would think she gave me encouragement.

Focus, I told myself. She's a total jerk, shouldn't be here. Pretend she's not.

BAL . . . me and the ball . . . *CO* . . . nothing else in the whole . . . *ho* . . . world. My shoulders twitched. I wanted to shove the ball down Goggles's throat.

"Let's go, Fire," the ref said.

"Savvy, two seconds," Gonzo said. "Go, girl. Go!"

I shot, missed. Our fans sighed their disappointment. On the block, Molly rubbed her hands down her shorts to dry her palms. Across from her, Bailey looked like she wanted to spit.

BAL-CO-ho.

Someone should tell them to stop. Only the Fire fans—way over on the far side of the gym—would understand what the chant meant. Even if they did hear, would anyone besides Aunt Betty actually come to my defense?

I laughed at the image of my aunt whacking Goggles across the knuckles with her cane.

I spun the ball, glanced over my shoulder at Gonzo. Her eyes narrowed, a cat coiling to strike. My teammates countered with their own encouragement. "Go, Savvy. Like you can. You can do it. Go, Fire."

My rabbit ears pointed the wrong way, hearing only one thing. *BAL-CO-ho.*

I missed the second shot. The Maya girl got the rebound. I blocked her pass, sending the ball into the corner, where Goggles and her trolls stood. Anyone watching would think the thumbs-up String Bean gave me was a sign of approval.

After bringing the ball in, Ice launched into a precision-passing play. I tried to go back to loving this game and admiring our worthy opponents, but I couldn't get Power's chant out of my head.

The shot clock ticked down. Her back to me, Maya shifted her shoulder to the left. My hand on her waist caught the lie and as she spun right, I moved with her.

I jumped so high, I stole the ball right out of Maya's hands. I passed it to Gonzo, who broke for the basket. Bubble took her pass and hit a sweet layup, making up for the two points I had missed at the free throw line.

I raced to the front court to celebrate with my teammates—

BAL-CO-ho.

—one step too late to grab Gonzo as she launched herself at Goggles.

CHAPTER THIRTY-FOUR

Gonzo knocked all three girls into the hall.

We all flew after her. Molly yanked String Bean off Gonzo's back while I pried Gonzo away from Goggles. Goggles thanked me with a pop in the nose. Bubble got into the mix, begging everyone to calm down while she kicked at a Power thug trying to climb my back.

The tournament director separated us, only to have Fire parents begin jawing with the Power parents who had come running from the concession table.

The head ref blasted the whistle until our eardrums practically exploded. He pointed at Fitz. "Take your team back to your bench until we settle this."

As we went back into the gym, Gonzo slipped her arm through mine. "I'm sorry."

"For what?" I said. "They deserved it."

She stopped, looked up at me. "I should have done this weeks ago."

I pressed the back of my hand into my nose to stop the bleeding. "Done what? Take on those turds like you actually know how to fight?"

"You know."

I did know. But I needed her to say it.

"Be the best friend ever."

Okay. Good. Yeah. "No need, Gonzo. You already own that one."

We sat together, back in the groove. On the opposite side of the scorer's table, the Ice players cast confused glances at us. With the Power and Fire parents still yelling out in the hall, word would get around soon enough.

Would this whole thing ever stop sucking?

The head ref talked to Ice for a minute, then came over to us. He pointed at Gonzo. "You're out of the game. You need to find your parents and go with them to speak to the director."

We groaned. Gonzo shushed us, squeezed my arm before leaving.

"North Middlesex has suggested you take ten minutes to settle your team, Coach. You don't deserve it, but Ice insisted."

Fitz herded us into the equipment room. "Either we play or we fight. You figure it out, gals. I'll be outside."

He slammed the door on his way out.

"Not fair," Molly said. "Those Power girls taunted us."

"You can't taunt if you're not in the game," Lori mumbled. "Nina went nuts. And we all know why."

"Yeah, okay. It's all my fault." I took a slow breath, let it out. "I should have quit last month when this all came down and left you guys out of it."

No one spoke. It didn't matter that all those blood tests had cleared me. The steroid accusation had skunked the whole team, leaving an odor that was impossible to get rid of.

"I could quit now," I said. "Or get you through this game and then quit."

Oh God, why didn't anyone say anything?

"Okay, I guess I'll finish this game. And then . . . you guys will do okay."

Molly kicked a bag of balls. "Don't be ridiculous, Savvy. You're not quitting."

The tears came, splattering my uniform shirt. "I wish I could explain why any of this happened but I can't. I am so sorry."

"Shut up, just shut up," Lori said. "This is all my fault."

Bubble gasped. "Those were your pills, Lori?"

"No, of course not. But I could have stopped this whole mess. My mother heard Savvy say she was on steroids. Bad enough—but then she saw the pills in her locker. I should have told her to forget it, that it wasn't our business, but I let her go ahead and talk to the tournament director." Lori covered her face. "I'm sorry. I screwed it up for everyone."

I should have known. Deep inside I had known she had something to do with this. Lori had said no when asked if she had snitched on me. Technically, that was correct—and Lori was all about technicalities.

Ava swore. Molly clenched her fists and Bailey glared openly. Like a breeze shifting over a garbage dump, the stink settled on Lori. I stared at her, holding back an ocean of anger. She met my gaze, open to whatever I would bring on her.

Ripping her head off wasn't enough payback for what I had been through.

The seconds ticked on. Staring at each other. No one speaking. Give her credit, Lori didn't look away. She had green eyes. How had I not known that?

This was my moment to man up and do the whole forgiveness thing. Michael Jordan said that to be successful, you have to be selfish. But once you get to your highest level, then you have to be unselfish.

This wasn't some kids' movie where someone comes off the bench to save the day, the star learns a lesson, and we all grow up to be wonderful citizens.

No friggin' way.

If Lori had backed me to her mother, I never would have been suspected, interrogated, suspended, and been called a *BALCO ho*.

Her eyes were green and one of her bottom teeth had a tiny chip. Wonder when that happened?

"Just tell me why," I said. "Why didn't you defend me?"

Lori looked me straight in the eye. "You waltzed onto this team with all the talent in the world. You work hard, I'll give you that. But you expect everything to come to you because you're blessed with all this ability. People like me have to do everything exactly right just to get a chance to compete. So when my mother asked me about those pills in your bag, I knew right away what they had to be. We've gone all over that in health class and athletic assemblies. I knew—and I was furious that you, with all the talent in the world, would cheat."

"I didn't."

"I know that now. I'm sorry." She threw up her hands. "I'll quit. You guys will do better without me."

I took a deep breath, willed myself to not boot her out the door. "We need you, Lori."

She shook her head. "You of all people don't need me, Savvy."

"We do. And I do."

"Don't patronize me."

"I'm not. You're my screen, remember? And now that Gonzo's been bounced from the game, who's gonna be my binkie?"

Lori covered her eyes.

"Come on, Lor," I said. "Please."

Fitz pounded on the door. "One minute," he yelled.

"We gotta go," Bubble said.

"Our fans await. Let's go." I put my arm around Lori, still hating her with every ounce of my being and yet determined to take the first step with her. Maybe the second step would be easier and on the third, I could just be annoyed.

Lori tried to smile, only managed a wince. "Your nose is bleeding."

I blew my nose on my shirt. "Okay, now that's taken care of, let's get out there."

We shuffled out of the room, all eyes on us.

"Savvy," Lori said.

"Yo."

"You're breaking the blood rule. Change your shirt. And hurry it up."

O≕O≕O≕O≕

The officials gave both teams five minutes to warm up. I shot for a couple, then stood near half-court, passing to my teammates. The Maya girl stood across the center line from me, doing the same.

"Hey," she said. "I heard about the . . . you know."

"Not true. I had the blood tests and all that."

"Yeah, some old lady came to our bench. She's so tall, she's got to be like your grandmother, right?"

"My father's aunt."

"Close enough. She showed us your blood tests."

I groaned. "Humiliate me, why doncha?"

She laughed. "Sucks to have to travel with those kinds of credentials. But I knew you were clean before your guard took on those jerks from Newport."

"How?"

"You got game, girl. Why screw it up with that garbage?"

I laughed. "Thanks. I'm Savvy, by the way. Savvy Christopher."

"I'm Diana," she said. "Diana Moore."

My eyes popped. "Ohmigosh. You got to be kidding. Any relation—?"

"To Maya? I wish."

The whistle blew.

"Good luck," Diana said.

"Back at you," I said. "Hey, wait up. Where you aiming for college?"

"Where else? Tennessee."

"Hey, I'll see ya there."

She laughed. "I'll save you a seat on the bench."

CHAPTER THIRTY-FIVE

With Diana Moore all over me, I scored only six points in the second half. Lori scored four points, Molly drained only one three-pointer. Bubble, who usually dished off to Gonzo, got hot and carried us to a win.

We had three games Sunday in the elimination round, and if we could survive—the championship on Monday.

I went home that night, still in shock. My blood churned every time I thought of Goggles and her stupid friends. Even worse was Lori's betrayal. Yeah, she felt bad and all that, but what was done was done. The whole thing sucked royally.

I had forgiven Lori on the outside, but my insides still squirmed. I went out and shot baskets. It was a whoppin' thirty degrees and getting colder by the minute. I worked the hoop until the anger cooled. I went inside, disgusted at the poor offerings of Saturday night television.

Callie was out with Alyssa somewhere. Aunt Betty was tuckered and went to bed. With my nerves still running on light speed, I sat down at the computer and Googled *BALCO*.

BALCO stood for the Bay Area Laboratory Cooperative, the company that the federal government had investigated in the steroid scandal. What a mess. Shot putters and sprinters. Football and baseball players. Chemists and trainers. Grand juries and trials. Accusations and denials. Tarnished reputations, best-selling books, and a couple of short prison stints resulted from it all.

Reporters and writers, senators and even the president had something to say on the matter. In the end, nothing changed—except for those marked with the stink.

Jason Giambi heard *BALCO* almost everywhere he played. He had admitted guilt, survived what might have been a steroid-spawned tumor, and was voted the American League's Comeback Player of the Year.

Home run king Barry Bonds heard *BALCO* everywhere he played. The guy sure looked like a juicer, but who was I to judge him? Too many people had assumed I was guilty too.

The whole thing made me sick.

When I typed in *Winstrol,* Google spit out tens of thousands of websites. The pills found in my bag were mild substances compared to the so-called designer steroids. I cringed at the word *injectables.* The thought of sticking a needle into my own butt or thigh was totally disgusting.

Sites educated parents about what to look for in their kids. After all the lectures, I could spout them in my sleep. Big muscles. Too many zits. Bursts of rage. In boys, shrunken testicles. That guys risk their manhood to improve their manhood was insane.

In girls, facial hair and a husky voice. My stomach twisted so hard, I thought I would throw up.

I took a deep breath, Googled *Winstrol* and *weight loss.* The computer flashed a multitude of hits.

A message board for female bodybuilders featured a running argument about using stanozolol to lose weight. Adding muscle means you gain weight, right? Not necessarily, some of the posters wrote. They said that, at least initially, you lost fat quickly because of a hyped-up metabolism. Their bottom line was: Take the juice to sculpt your body, and the fat takes care of itself.

It hit me like a sucker punch to the head. The answer had been in front of us the whole time and we all missed it.

I went outside and waited for my sister to come home.

○⊪○⊪○⊪○⊪

I sat in the dark, wondering why.

I suffered and my sister said nothing. Mom and Dad suffered with me and she said nothing. Marc was interrogated, humiliated, tested, and she said nothing.

Finally, headlights came up the drive. Callie got out, said good night to Alyssa and a couple others. When she came up on the porch, I tapped her on the shoulder. "Callie."

"Savvy, what the hell? You scared the crap out of me."

"We have to talk."

"Not now. I'm going to bed."

I grabbed her arm. "No."

Panic flickered in her eyes. "I'm tired. We'll talk tomorrow."

"Now."

"It's freezing out here," she whispered.

"I know," I said.

"Then we should go inside, right?"

"Not that." I locked my hands on her shoulder and stared down at her. "I know, Callie. *I know.*"

She went limp.

"Why?" I said.

She bit her lip so hard, I thought she'd bleed.

"Callie, you've got to tell me." Tears rolled down my cheeks. I hated that I had to beg her. "Please tell me why."

She stepped back, in a full cringe as if I had whipped her. "You're strong, Savvy. Strong in all the best ways. I knew you'd be okay."

"I wasn't okay, though. Was I?"

"I knew you would be and look—you are. But you know I just can't . . ."

"Oh, stop already with the whole victim thing."

"I try, Savvy. You know I try."

"Wanna know what I know, Callie?"

She gazed at me with big eyes.

"All those times I said I hated you?" I said. "When we were fighting over the room or using the phone or dumb things? I never really meant that I hated you."

"I know," she said.

I picked up my basketball and rested my cheek against it like a security blanket.

"But now I hate you for real," I said. "For real. And forever."

Callie opened the front door, stood framed in the porch light like a ghost. "For all it's worth, Savvy? I hate myself too."

CHAPTER THIRTY-SIX

I woke up in the middle of the night with a blasting headache. I went to the bathroom, took a couple Tylenol, and returned to our bedroom. Still ready to erupt, I decided to wake Callie up and remind her how much I hated her.

The top bunk was empty. On her pillow was a note that said: *I needed to get some fresh air. I'm so sorry.*

I slipped on sweatpants and a coat, and went outside. Callie wasn't on the porch, in the driveway, or in the barn. One in the morning—where could she be?

Let her play drama queen. I went back to bed, tossed and turned for twenty minutes. Screw her, I thought.

But what if this wasn't an act?

I rang Alyssa's cell, woke her, and got yelled at. I mustered up the same courage, called Marc, and got cursed out. I went back out on the front porch and waited. Cold seeped into me. The moon was full and high, casting a fake daylight over everything.

What should I do?

Call my parents in New York. They'd pack up and be back here by breakfast. Stupid idea. Ten minutes after I woke them up, Callie would appear.

Wake up Aunt Betty? What could she do that I couldn't?

Call the cops? On television they said they couldn't do anything for twenty-four hours. Besides, there was no threat in *I need to get some fresh air*.

Why was I even out here? Callie didn't give a flip about how I had suffered. I should be sleeping. Fire's first game was at noon. Thanks a bunch, sister, for ruining what little season I had left.

Manny barked from the low pasture. Was she out there, or were those bloody coyotes on the prowl?

Some detective I was. I hadn't even asked Callie where she got the pills. Marc had tested clean, but maybe it was another one of the football players, or a juicer at her gym. What if she had gone to warn her supplier? But all she'd need to do was call.

Manny barked again. I grabbed a flashlight and headed for the pasture. The moonlight was so bright, I didn't need the flashlight. The sheep huddled in a fuzzy clump, keeping close for warmth and protection. As I got close, Manny growled.

"It's me," I said.

He quieted, sat at the edge of the flock, waiting to see what I wanted. How about a puppy hug, you dope?

I walked him around the perimeter of the fence, calling Callie's name. The birches stood high above me on the hill, their slender trunks shimmering in the silver night.

I leashed Manny and took him out to the street with me. Away from the open fields, the night turned spooky. Tree branches cast twisted shadows, and dead silence hung over the road.

Worry tickled the back of my neck. Had I driven Callie

to something desperate? Stupid, stupid, stupid—why hadn't I just waited for Mom and Dad to come home?

Only a saint could have waited.

I'd give Callie another ten minutes, then I'd wake up Aunt Betty.

We went back to the fields and hiked up to the high pasture. After we moved the sheep to the low pasture three weeks ago, Callie had started coming up here to have some privacy. Just taking walks, Callie said, but I knew it was to get away from me. And now I knew why.

"Callie? Callie!"

Not even a whisper of wind. Just silence.

If getting cut from cheering had scared my sister into taking steroids, my discovering the truth must have completely terrified her. Had she really come outside for some fresh air? Had she run away?

Or did she hate herself enough to do something desperate?

○=○=○=○=

Two o'clock in the morning. Aunt Betty brewed a pot of tea while I spilled out my story.

"It crossed my mind that she was the one who had stuck the pills in my bag," I said. "But I assumed she was hiding them for Marc. And when he tested clean, I didn't give it another thought. The answer was right in front of me—"

"In front of all of us," Aunt Betty said. "All this to be trim and fit. I had hoped in this new millennium women would know better."

"What do we do?"

Aunt Betty sat down with a groan. Her leg still hurt until she got fully warmed up. "The Bouchards have Alyssa calling around to her friends. If she doesn't find Callie among any of them, we'll call the police."

"No, we can't. Okay, maybe we should. I don't know." I grabbed my head, tried to keep it from blasting off my shoulders. "If we call the cops, the whole thing might come out."

"Calliope was the one foolish enough to obtain these pills. You were the victim in this."

Callie had played the victim her whole life. Now that I was in the role, I realized how much it stunk.

"I'm going back out there," I said.

Aunt Betty shook her head. "You don't have to do this alone, Savannah."

"I drove her away," I said. "I'll find her."

"Savannah, it's all right to ask for help."

The usual arguments pretzeled around my brain. Mom and Dad were too stressed and needed their weekend away. Aunt Betty was still hobbled from her accident. I could call Gonzo, but what could she do?

My chest tightened, a knot that I tried to cough up but it got stuck in my throat. It was impossible to think straight with anger and fear strangling me. I put my head down on the table, wishing I could sink into the wood, because that's how dumb and useless I felt.

Aunt Betty touched my hair. "Savvy . . ."

I grabbed the phone and punched in my mother's phone number. After many rings, my father answered.

"Daddy," I said. "I need you."

229

In fifth grade, we to had to memorize a poem by Robert Frost about the New England woods.

The woods are lovely, dark, and deep.
But I have miles to go before I sleep.

In New Mexico the closest thing we got to woods was three cacti in a row. Snow was far away, on the mountaintops.

I got the poem now—except for the lovely part. The woods were dark and deep, even with the moon shining through the bare trees. Farther in, the huge pine trees blocked all light so the woods became a black hole.

As I stood at the stone wall, that darkness terrified me.

Deep in those woods were fisher cats, porcupines, skunks, squirrels, rabbits—some trying to kill and the rest trying to survive the night. Owls cruising the darkness with daylike vision. Coyotes in the brush, sniffing out fresh meat.

Monsters of the night. Monsters of my mind.

What black hole had Callie disappeared into? I couldn't just sit around and wait for my parents to get home. It was almost a four-hour trip back from New York.

The sheep clustered so tightly in the low pasture that they looked like one animal instead of almost a hundred. Aunt Betty said that clumping was a natural defense against predators. Even so, coyotes or mountain lions or wolves would try to find a weak one and divide it from the flock.

Drive it apart and devour it while the others huddled in fear.

Manny's job was to make sure that didn't happen. Four

lambs had been lost this fall, but he had gotten stronger, bigger, and smarter. It was in him to defend sheep, goats, even cattle with his life.

It was in me to jump for the sky and shoot the stars out.

How could Callie let my one thing be taken from me? If she was out in those dark, deep woods, she deserved to be. Except—that one thing that was basketball turned out to be neither the beginning nor end of my world.

There was another thing that was more a part of me than blocking a shot or driving for the basket. Another *one thing* that kept my mother going when all hope had run out. The same thing that had wounded my sister when she saw our father fall from the roof and lie broken on the ground. The same thing that made Dad struggle up off the ground and endure pain few could. The same thing that prompted Aunt Betty to open her home to us. The same thing that drove me to learn to love sheep.

My family was the one thing that would kill me to lose.

I tightened my grip on Manny's leash and walked into the woods to find my sister.

CHAPTER THIRTY-SEVEN

When I got scared, Manny let me put my arms around him. Maybe he thought I was one of his sheep, or maybe he thought I was a big idiot. Didn't matter—he was big and warm and there for me.

We followed the trails until the sky turned pink. We didn't find any coyotes or dead lambs or monsters. No Callie either.

We backtracked, Manny sniffing out the right path when I forgot whether I had turned left or right. When I spotted the barn through the trees, I knew we were almost home.

Manny and I trudged down the dirt road, the rising sun at our back. The frost stretched out before us like a carpet of diamonds. I gave him one last hug and released him into the low pasture. The sheep nosed the frozen grass, wanting to graze. I needed to bring some hay out for them.

As I passed the hay shed, Callie stepped out.

When my heart finally stopped hammering, I said, "Where the hell have you been?"

"I walked to the police station."

"You went to the cops?" I said.

"No. Just the police station. I chickened out from going in."

"And what the freakin' hell do you want me to do now? Congratulate you for your *almost*?"

She scuffed the ground. "Mom and Dad are here."

"Thank God. I called them."

"Did you tell them?"

"No. You get to do that," I said over that knot of anger in my throat.

She toed the dirt so hard, she made a hole. "I can't."

My legs felt like dead tree stumps, and my head throbbed. Exhaustion soaked my body like sweat. I didn't have the strength to even look at her anymore.

"Savvy."

I can't, I thought, *can't and won't.* But I looked at her anyway.

"Maybe I can tell them," Callie whispered. "Maybe I can, if you just come with me."

"Let's go." I took a step and stumbled, almost fell on my face.

My sister took my arm and together we went to the house.

The pills were Alyssa's idea.

No wonder she told me to hang in after they were found. No wonder she told Maddie to be nice to me. She didn't want anything coming back on her.

Mom squinted, as if unable to visualize this news. "But Alyssa is so nice."

"Don't you get it? That's why she did it," Callie said. "She was *helping* me."

Aunt Betty hobbled around the table, putting out orange juice and toast that no one seemed in any mood to eat. "I'm not sure I comprehend how giving a young girl drugs is being nice."

My father rubbed the stubble on his chin, making a *spfft spfft* noise. "Was she taking them too?"

"Sometimes."

"I don't understand."

"Girls use short cycles to firm up for tryouts or sports. Sometimes after injuries. Alyssa did a cycle once for a month before a photo shoot. Better than diet pills, she says, because they get you into shape. It's not like those nasty weight-lifting women. We take them in small doses, just enough to help us buff up."

"Are you still taking them?" Mom asked.

She shook her head.

"Why didn't you get rid of them?"

"They cost seventy bucks. And . . ." Callie grabbed a paper towel, soaked up her tears. ". . . I thought I might need them again."

"Why did you put them in my bag?" My question came out like a growl.

"After the diet pill thing went down, Mom and Dad searched my stuff all the time. Your gym bag was one place I knew they wouldn't look. You would never disturb that sock shrine of yours. I'm sorry, Savvy."

I called her the foulest swear I could come up with.

My mother was shocked. "Savvy, don—"

"Terri, you stop. Savvy has the right," my father said.

"Where did Alyssa get them?" Aunt Betty asked.

"A trainer at the gym. I think he gets them on the Internet."

"Damn coyotes."

"You have to tell Detective Carrod," I said.

Callie stood, glancing left and right like a trapped squirrel. "I can't."

"You have to."

"Mom, Dad, please. You tell them. I can't."

"No," my father said. "You can and you will."

Mom dialed her cell phone. Then she handed it to Callie and said, "Talk. Now."

○=○=○=○=

The commissioner suspended Gonzo for the rest of the tournament. Sitting with her parents, she wore makeup, a nice top and jeans, her hair in a red scrunchie to show Fire pride.

Kronos grabbed me as I went in to use the bathroom. Goggles, String Bean, and the other BALCO-chanter was with her. "My girls want to apologize."

I caught Goggles's smirk as she stood behind her coach. No way was this her idea.

"No," I said. "They don't need to."

"I insist on it," Kronos said.

"You're the one who should apologize, not them. You teach them to play right on that edge and when they go over, you pretend you don't see it."

"I understand why you're upset, Savvy. But you're still young. Couple of years—you'll see how the game is supposed to be played."

"No wonder they're thugs—with a coach like you."

She stiffened. "I'm sorry you see it that way."

"I'm glad I do."

Kronos turned and walked away, her players following.

Goggles gave me the finger behind her back. I just laughed.

Ten minutes later, Fire gathered in a quiet corner for our girls-only meeting.

"What do we do now?" Molly said. "Without Gonzo?"

"We'll be all right." The catch in Bubble's voice said otherwise.

Why was everyone looking at me? I was a shooter and blocker—not a leader. The silence was painful as we all waited for someone to step up.

Talent wins games, Michael Jordan said. But teamwork and intelligence wins championships. I stared at Lori. She was the oldest on the team, and probably the only girl who even thought about leadership.

She blinked, looked down at her hands, and back at me.

I gave her a nod and a smile.

"Bubble is right," Lori said. "We will be okay. We just need to stick with the game plan. Ava will fill in for Nina just fine."

"I can't move the ball like Gonzo," Ava said.

"So we'll run more passing plays. We just need to be sure to be where we need to be for each other.

"Yeah," Molly said. "Okay. That'll work."

Bailey looked at me. Not convinced.

"Lori's right," I said. "We'll be better than okay."

We circled up, hands clasped.

"One last thing. I'll screen for Savvy on offense. And the rest of you . . ." Lori grinned. "Feed Christopher like she ain't eaten for a week."

CHAPTER THIRTY-EIGHT

We beat the Newport Power in the semifinal game of the Veteran's Day qualifier. I finessed Goggles, made more layups from my left side than my right, and had a double-double.

We lost in the finals, missing a trip to Orlando by two points. We were all so emotionally exhausted, we didn't much care.

On Tuesday, Detective Carrod questioned Alyssa, offered her immunity, and got enough information to arrest the guy at the gym. Someone put up a blog called CallieSnitch .blogspot.com, when my sister got out that she had talked to the cops. My sister got nasty e-mails and calls, even a couple of death threats.

Callie not only refused to go to school, she wouldn't get out of bed. She didn't speak for a week, even after a shrink made a house call. She ran out of the room, found me in the driveway, and held on to me for dear life.

"We'll take care of her," I told the psychologist, though I had no idea how.

Another week passed. Callie didn't talk, barely ate, and had no interest in her iPod. When she wasn't in bed, she was at the pasture, staring at the sheep.

Aunt Betty and I paid a visit to George Otis, explained the problem.

We came home with Manny's brother. The runt of the litter, Pete hadn't sold. Unlike his bigger brother, Pete got to come into the house, get hugs and kisses, jump around, and be a silly pet.

He was also allowed to sleep in my bedroom. The day after we got him, I found him in the top bunk with Callie. She had to have lifted him up there because—runt or not—this dog was no flier.

"Is that okay?" she asked me. "I know he's your dog."

"Manny's my dog," I said. "You runts gotta stick together."

That night Callie came downstairs, raging and sobbing that she'd never go to school again. What looked like a massive freak show was actually a sign of mental health.

Aunt Betty solved the school issue by volunteering to tutor Callie until she felt strong enough to go back to school. Like that was ever going to happen.

Strangely, the crap didn't roll downhill to me at Taylor Middle School. Maddie kept her distance, maybe trying to keep Alyssa's role in all this out of circulation. Gonzo and I made the basketball team, we clobbered Taylor's biggest rival in our first game, and the kids who had dumped on me all fall were now my biggest fans.

On the last day of November, Fish Face—Derek—asked me to the winter dance. My first impulse was to tell him what a stupid loser he was, as was my second, third, and infinite impulse. I chewed my lip, casting in the back of my mind for the *what would Michael Jordan do* bit of wisdom.

Everyone from M.J. to Maya Moore to Kevin Garnett

knows one truth: A player is great only if he or she elevates everyone around them.

I smiled at Derek and said, "Hey, thanks. I can't because I've got some family stuff going on that night. But if you want to come out to the farm sometime, check out our sheep and stuff, that would be cool."

"Can I come tomorrow?"

Grief, I thought. I've still got a lot to learn.

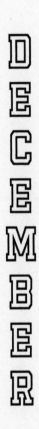

DECEMBER

CHAPTER THIRTY-NINE

The second week of December, Callie officially withdrew from the high school. Molly said that Alyssa was more popular than ever—playing the victim role for all it was worth. Then a cheating scandal broke out and everyone forgot the whole steroid thing.

The home-schooling thing with Aunt Betty was supposed to be temporary. Even my sister admitted she had to get back into the world. We couldn't afford a private school, not while my parents still had creditors to pay off.

Jennifer Kronos stepped in to help. Even though I had no interest in talking to her, she kept in touch with Mom. She knew of a good private school in Providence that was looking for a golf coach.

My father took the job in exchange for tuition. A few days before Christmas, Callie started classes. When she got home that evening, she already had two phone calls from new friends and my father had a new bounce in his step.

Back in the game, Mom said. Passing his sweet swing on to the next generation.

O⸱O⸱O⸱O⸱

Molly and Bailey were annoyed because I hadn't seen them play high school varsity yet. I had gone to the charter school to see Lori and Olivia play, and the vocational school to see

Bubble and Ava. No way was I going to the high school. The thought of running into Alyssa or any of her friends put me in a panic.

"You have to," Gonzo said.

Aunt Betty caught wind of my refusal. "Are you too chicken to go to watch your friends?"

Ouch.

I went to the next home game with a Red Sox cap pulled low on my face. Like I could actually disguise myself at six feet three inches?

There was not a cool kid in sight. The crowd was made up of family and friends. I felt comfortable enough to take off my hat and enjoy the game. Partway through the first half, I had to pee.

Coming out of the restroom, I ran into Marc Sardakis.

I gulped, almost fainted before I got up the courage to say, "I'm sorry."

He rolled his eyes and walked away.

I ran after him and grabbed his arm. "I mean it. I'm sorry for what we put you through."

"Whatever." He yanked away. "What you and your parents did to me was nothing to what your friggin' sister did."

"I know, Marc. She did it to me too. Because she was scared."

He sighed, leaned against the wall. "Aren't we all?"

I leaned with him, staring up at the ceiling. "Why?"

"Because if you're good but not quite good enough, you get all sorts of advice on how to get better. Kids work their tail off and still they're not in the mix. So they try whatever they can, because coaches and parents are telling them they're almost there."

I nodded, thinking of Lori.

"And if you're like you and me," Marc said, "you hear from the time you're a little kid how wonderful you are. You know it, because on the field or the court, you're the star. Once you're on top, it's scary to think about being anywhere else."

"Yeah, and you still have to get better," I said. "Because the competition only gets more fierce."

Marc slid his arm around my shoulders. "Sometimes it sucks to be us."

I put my arm around his waist in the same way I might do with Gonzo. "I'm sorry for accusing you. Really. I was scared out of my mind."

"Yeah, okay. I know." He gave me a little squeeze. "Someone said your sister was having a nervous breakdown."

"She's okay now. Going to a new school."

"Okay. Good." Marc stepped away. "Well, I've got to get going."

"I'm so sor—"

"Hey, I got it, it's done, we're moving on." Marc gave me a wave, headed down the hall. After a couple steps, he turned around. "Savvy. You're not going to bag it like your sister, right? You're coming here next year, right?"

"I guess. Sure."

"Cool. See you, Hotshot."

I watched him go, my heart too worn out to thunder after him.

Callie and I cut a Christmas tree deep in the woods and put it up in the bay window. Every day when I got off the bus, Aunt Betty made sure the lights were on so I could see it as I walked up the driveway.

Snow fell the weekend before Christmas. Mr. Otis plowed the driveway and made sure my basketball court was clear. Betty made him coffee and they chatted about how the only farm store in town was going out of business.

"They ever gonna hook up?" Callie wondered.

"Probably not. They got things how they want 'em," I said.

Christmas morning we gathered around the tree and opened presents. I was thrilled to get a mall gift certificate from my parents. Since I was officially six three and a half now, my jeans were all high-water.

Aunt Betty passed me a present. "Hope you like it," she said.

"You shouldn't have," I said, but ripped through the paper. It was a Lady Vols warm-up suit.

"Ohmigosh," I squealed. "Where'd you get it?"

"George Otis showed me how to order things online. I expect I shall be spending far too much time on eBay now."

We got Aunt Betty new rubber boots from L.L.Bean. She clapped her hands with glee. "The best gift. I so needed these."

Callie and I pooled our money to buy Mom and Dad a gift certificate to a weekend getaway on Martha's Vineyard.

When everything under the tree was opened, I stood up, now impossible to miss in my Tennessee orange.

"Rumor is Santa left a gift for Callie," I said, and dragged out a long, heavy box from behind the sofa.

"What's this?" she said.

"How would I know? Do I look like Santa?"

Aunt Betty was the Santa. She had insisted on paying me for the work I had done all fall. She wouldn't take my *no* for any sort of an answer. After putting aside a thousand bucks for going to a national tournament next spring, there had been plenty of money to buy my sister the kind of present Mom and Dad couldn't.

"Golf clubs?" Callie said. "Savvy, you shouldn't—"

I cut Callie off before she could go goo-ey on me. "This is on Santa, not me."

"Santa's one smart dude," Dad said.

"Especially since we have a golf coach in the family," Mom said. "What do you think, Cal? You had a great stroke when you were little."

"The school needs some good women golfers." Dad grinned—he had already stuck the schedule on our refrigerator.

I held my breath, waiting for my sister's answer. We all knew she'd never shake another pom-pom. Gymnastics might have been a possibility, but her new school didn't have a team. Even if she could toss a ball or swing a bat, Callie wasn't much for team sports.

"Yeah. I think I would," she finally said. "Thanks . . . um, Santa."

"You'll be good," Dad said.

"Really good," I said, and meant it.

"Savvy, feel free to borrow them," Callie said. "If you're ever in the mood to be Michelle Wie."

"Thanks, but I'll stick to being LeBron James," I said. Without the testosterone, of course.